SAM CRESCENT

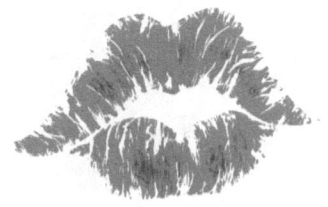

EVERNIGHT PUBLISHING ®

www.evernightpublishing.com

Editor: Karyn White

Cover Artist: Jay Aheer

ISBN: 978-1-77339-795-5

SAM CRESCENT

PLAIN JANE AND THE MAFIA BEAST

Sam Crescent

Copyright © 2018

Chapter One

"This will not be easy for you," said Vincenzo Barbato, killer for the mafia and expert within his field. He worked for the Galiza family, the most feared mafia family in the world, and he was their tool. The one they used to dispatch, hunt, torture, and kill without remorse. Since birth he'd had a knack for … killing.

He'd been found by the Galiza as a child in an orphanage when complaints about what he did to hurt people were heard by the grandfather of the family. He was adopted by them soon after their first visit to the orphanage. The people who'd been taking care of him just wanted the weird-ass kid out of their lives. From the moment he was adopted, he was made aware he would in no way inherit or be part of the mafia as a boss. That was strictly for family only, and Galiza had plenty of sons. Vincenzo would always be a tool. Someone they respected and used but could also be dispensed with. As the years progressed, his skills became defined, until he was the monster everyone feared. The mafia's beast.

There was no secret he couldn't discover, no truth that could be hidden from him. He loved his work, relished it even.

"Please, please, I was told the Galiza family was finished. That they were being overturned."

"And who told you that?" Vincenzo asked.

He watched.

Waited.

And he saw the man dying a little inside.

Holding his hand out, the man struggled, but Vincenzo was far stronger. The man's struggles were useless as he grabbed a pair of garden shears used to snap branches and cut a single finger off. The screams began, but that was fine. Next, Vincenzo grabbed some pliers, and for the other three fingers and thumb, he pulled the nails out of their beds.

At some point, the man passed out, and Vincenzo stood back, wiping his hands.

"Please tell me to never get on your bad side," Daniel said.

Daniel was his guard, not that he needed one, but Galiza demanded he have one. Vincenzo took care of himself, and Daniel was a respected solider within the mafia business.

"It is what it is," he said.

"Don't you ever, you know, vomit?"

"Not anymore."

"Did you ever?" Daniel asked.

He smiled. "No."

"I thought so. You're a freaky fucker." Daniel pointed at the man on the floor. "What about him? What do you think his deal is?"

"Loyalty was tested and he failed. There's someone who is trying to rise up against the Galiza, and it's my job to find out who."

"I still can't believe anyone would be dumb enough to try this." Daniel released a breath. "It's a good job I didn't eat."

"Weak stomach?"

"It's not the blood but the screaming. It's giving me a headache."

"You sound like a girl."

"I don't know how you can do it, man. All you got to do is pop 'em. One bullet to the head and they're gone. No noise to deal with."

"That's why I am who I am, and you're you."

"Ah, you're, like, a king, and me, I'm just a piece of shit?" Daniel asked.

They were always joking about their place within the mafia. Neither of them had any real place. If Galiza decided to end his life, then he'd be dead. At the moment, he was useful. He made sure that no one could get rid of him.

"How much longer?" Daniel glanced down at his watch.

"You got somewhere to be?"

"Not really, but I'd like to eat after all of this."

"And you think I'm the sick fuck."

Vincenzo grabbed the bucket of water and threw it at the man in the chair, who came to, gasping.

"Names?" Vincenzo said.

"I don't know any."

For the next hour he tortured the man until he'd gotten every single name of the men and women who were part of the organization. Once it was done, he slit the man's throat and proceeded to clean up everything.

Daniel arranged for the cleaner they used to take the body and dispose of it. The warehouse was cleaned down, and Vincenzo walked out without a backward glance.

"So, I'm thinking Chinese."

"Not happening. We're going to Fabio's," Vincenzo said.

"Dude, we always go there. Don't you like anything other than pasta?"

"What's the point in eating anything else? Pasta is the best thing there is."

Daniel sighed. "Just once, okay. Can we, like, vote on it?"

"You really want to do rock, paper, scissors on where we eat?"

"Come on, man. You've got to give me something. Getting older is not easy on a guy." Daniel grabbed his stomach. "It takes a lot to look this good."

"It looks like you could visit the gym a few times, my friend. You're getting a little ... big."

"Screw you, Vincenzo. I'm still the one with the ladies, and you have yet to find anyone to keep around."

"I don't need to keep anyone around when I can have them when and where I want them. That's the power I have at being me." He also wouldn't keep a woman around.

Over the years, he'd seen more betrayals than anyone else. Women were weak. They were vulnerable, and a lot of them worked with their pussy. He didn't need a woman in his life. He visited a couple of regular women who had no problem servicing his cock when he needed it.

There were no attachments, and he was under no illusions that they saw many men, most of them members of the mafia. He didn't have a problem with that. He wasn't possessive. No woman had ever made him feel possessive in the least.

"Come on, man, one go. If you win, I won't ask again. If I win, we go somewhere else, and we can eat wherever you want for the next month," Daniel said.

This man was the closest thing he'd ever had to a friend. He'd stuck around for two years, which was longer than the last one, who he ended up putting a bullet in after only a day. He went through a lot of guards, which was his argument that he didn't need one.

Daniel was different.

He didn't look at him like a freak, nor was his loyalty focused elsewhere. He was part of the Galiza family and had no interest in killing the men that fed him.

They were … friends.

So, instead of beating him at rock, paper, scissors, Vincenzo let him win, and lo and behold, he decided to pick a greasy, old-fashioned diner as somewhere to eat.

He hated greasy food.

"You complain about your weight and we're eating here?" Vincenzo said.

"Come on, pasta is full of carbs."

"Burgers and fried chicken aren't?" he asked.

"Okay, there's a girl I like and she works here. Also, I like the fried chicken and the pecan pie. It's to die for."

"I could just kill you now," Vincenzo said.

"Come on, pretend to be human for one minute."

"Fine. Fine. Let's go and eat your precious food." He didn't mind going to the gym tomorrow. It was his off day.

Climbing out of the car, he walked up to the diner that had a lot of people inside. This was a surprise. Diners were … old. He didn't expect them to be so popular. Entering the diner, he had to admit it smelled really good, which again, was a surprise.

He followed Daniel's lead, aware of people staring at them. They were well-known wherever they went. Working for the mafia there was always a crowd of whispers. He didn't mind and rather liked that no one would mess with him.

Taking a seat in the center of the diner, he picked up the menu.

"Don't worry, the waitress will come and read out the specials," Daniel said.

"What is this waitress's name?" He didn't give a shit about the woman. All he wanted was some food.

"Rachel."

Daniel was clearly pussy-whipped, as he was spending more time looking around than paying any real attention.

"Hi, guys, sorry about the wait. I'm Arika, and I'm here to take your order."

Vincenzo looked at the young woman with sad brown eyes and long brown hair that was pulled up into a ponytail. She didn't have any makeup on, and to many, he figured she looked kind of plain. There was nothing striking about her. Nothing to make men give a second look, only, Vincenzo liked looking at her. There was something about her eyes.

There was a darkness swirling in her gaze as she waited to hear what they wanted to order.

"Where's Rachel?" Daniel asked.

"She doesn't work Wednesday nights. I'm sorry," Arika said. "Would you like me to tell you the specials?"

Vincenzo saw Daniel had lost interest, but he hadn't. He wanted to eat, and he wasn't about to be moved because his friend hadn't gotten what he wanted.

"What's the specials?"

"We've got our house special fried chicken, the three-meat burger, and also the lasagna is pretty good too. The pecan pie is the best and award-winning as well," she said.

Her voice.

It was so soft.

He could gladly listen to her all day.

"That's okay, we'll take cof—"

"I'll have the three-meat burger please," Vincenzo said, cutting off his friend. Giving him a pointed look, he waited for his friend to order, and once that was complete, he watched her walk away.

She was on the bigger side, but that was more than okay with him. He liked women with curves; nice full tits, rounded ass; perfect body for him to grab onto and fuck. It had been a long time since a woman made him feel this way, and certainly never a plain woman.

"We could leave," Daniel said.

"Why would I do that? I want to stay and eat."

****

Arika Jane tried to hide the wince as she grabbed the large coffee jug and made her way around the room, filling coffee, taking dishes back and forth. She'd been on a twelve-hour shift, and it was close to the end. Her feet were killing her. She just wanted to curl up, eat some noodles, and do the last of her English essay for college. If she got lucky, she'd find the extra energy to also start studying for a final as well.

Rachel's "lover boy" had turned up again.

She knew for a fact that Rachel wanted nothing to do with the guy as she'd purposefully gone out of her way to change shifts just to avoid him. It didn't bother Arika. She could work her schedule either way.

Once she finished wiping down several tables, she walked to the two men that she'd heard nothing but whispers about all night.

"They're part of the mafia."

"Don't look."

"He'll kill you."

"Deadly."

"Dangerous."

"Mafia."

"Can I get you two anything?" she asked.

"Do you have Rachel's number?" the guy who'd become creepy stalker dude asked.

"I can't give out numbers of employees, sorry."

"How about if I make it worth your while?"

She stared at the twenty he slid across to her.

Shaking her head, she turned to the guy that remained quiet. "Is there anything else I can get you?"

"The check would be lovely, Arika."

She didn't like that he knew her name but knew there was nothing she could do about it. Her name tag told him what he needed to know. Arika Jane. The name she'd been given at birth when she'd been dropped off by an unknown person. No way of knowing who she belonged to, not that it mattered.

They hadn't cared about her, and rather than dwell on the family that didn't care, she focused on her education. She'd been a plain kid growing up, never catching any family's eye, so she didn't anticipate being adopted.

She'd stayed in the system from birth until she was sent out into the world at eighteen. Since then it had been one battle after another.

She brought the men their check and took their plates and other dishes. A few minutes later, the man brought the check back to her to cash.

"Everything was stunning, thank you." He held the check and money out to her, and she took it. Glancing down, she saw a hundred-dollar tip.

"This must be a mistake."

"Your service was exceptional, even if my friend

made you nervous. Thank you. I will be coming again."

She tried to give him the tip back, but he wouldn't take it. When he glared at her, fear shot down her spine and she nodded, quickly pocketing the money.

"Have a nice night, Arika."

Watching him leave the diner made her nervous. She didn't like the way he kept looking at her. She was used to being overlooked, but that man, whoever he was, looked right at her.

He saw her, and she didn't like exactly how deep he seemed to be able to see.

The next thirty minutes went by in a blur. She helped clean up, as that was part of her job, and then it was time for her to leave. Grabbing her jacket, as it was cold out, and slinging her bag over her shoulder, she entered the cold evening night.

She held the strap of her bag, staring down at the ground. The city was not the best place to be, and she found not lingering near dirty, empty alleyways was the best way of staying alive. She didn't want to die, had no reason to.

She may not have experienced the best start in life, but she worked every single day to turn her life around, and she rather loved what she did. Working her ass off, she had her own rented apartment and worked as many classes as she could at a local campus, constantly paying off those lessons so she was never in debt.

Even if she was sick, she'd try to find homemade remedies to make sure she didn't overspend.

With careful planning she knew she'd have a good life. Once she had a career and enough savings, she intended to help kids in the foster system like her. Kids that were not loved but needed someone to care about more than looking right in the family. Not that she thought all parents were like that, but it just felt like it at times.

"You watch your fucking mouth."

Head bowed, she tried to ignore the anger that she heard, and in the next second, gunshots exploded and pain seared her abdomen, taking her breath away. She'd been crossing the road, facing an alleyway as she did so.

Putting a hand to her side, she gasped at the excruciating pain, stumbling as everything seemed to swirl around her. She couldn't keep her balance, and she collapsed onto the ground.

She'd been shot.

Falling to the ground, she couldn't seem to move.

The pain was unbearable.

"You think you can run your mouth and get away with it. This is for the Galiza family."

She gasped as another shot rang out.

The sound of footsteps advanced on her.

Tears filled her eyes.

The two men from the diner.

The two that were part of the mafia.

One of them held a gun. The other looked pissed.

"Shit, it's the waitress from the diner," the one asking after Rachel said.

Arika didn't want to die.

"We need to get rid of her."

The one who'd seen her crouched near her side, his hand moving the bag out of the way, then the coat.

"She got shot."

"She's a fucking liability, Vince. You know what you've got to do."

She took a shaking breath as he moved her hand away.

"It's bad," Vince said.

She stared into his blue eyes, seeing the evil lurking beneath.

He tilted his head to the side.

"This wasn't her fault."

"Drag her into the damn alley and be done with her. Let her bleed out. Or cut her fucking thigh and let nature take its course."

"I'm not going to fucking kill her," Vince said.

His words snapped out, and she tensed up.

"I don't want to die," she said.

"You will if I don't take you with me."

"Vince, you can't take her."

Tears leaked out of her eyes, tracing down into her hair. Dying right now was not part of her plan. She sniffled and gritted her teeth as she stared up at the dark sky.

Now was not supposed to happen.

She gasped as he stroked her cheek.

Staring into his eyes, she didn't know what he was thinking or what he saw when he looked at her.

"For fuck's sake, Vince, let me deal with it."

She cried out as his friend pointed the gun at her.

Closing her eyes, she flinched, wishing and praying that he didn't pull that fucking trigger.

"Please, please, please," she said, whispering the words.

"What the fuck, Vince?"

She opened her eyes and saw Vince hold the man's arm. He'd twisted the gun and it was now pointed at the man who'd been about to kill her.

"She's not going to die. Not tonight." He got to his feet, and she gasped as he put his hands beneath her body, lifting her up.

At first, she tensed up, afraid of what was about to happen.

"Are you fucking shitting me right now? She's got to die. You can't take her to Galiza's home."

"I'm taking her home with me. I'll deal with her there."

"Are you fucking mental right now? That is not going to happen."

"Daniel, I put up with all your shit, but now is not the time to question me." He stopped, and her head rested against his shirt.

Everything was getting a little blurry, and she was starting to feel sick. The pain was there, swallowing her whole.

She took a deep breath, which burned inside her, and cried out as he jolted.

He started to shout, but she didn't make out any words.

Closing her eyes, she just wanted to fall asleep.

Her feet hurt.

Everywhere hurt.

Would it be so wrong to fall asleep in this man's arms?

Dying a virgin would suck, but in his arms, that would be pretty amazing actually. There was something about Vince. He terrified and aroused her.

Piqued her interest and now she was going to die.

Such a shame.

It would have been interesting to see just how much of a monster he was.

Chapter Two

"You know they'll kill her," Daniel said.

"Why don't you shut the fuck up?" Vince watched as the doctor removed the bullet from the woman's abdomen.

This was the doctor he came to whenever he needed anything done without paperwork or attention. This man knew how to get everything done, and they'd worked together for a long time.

Doctor Alverez.

He'd been a little confused when he brought a woman here, but that was the point of paying the fee.

Arika was out of it. He held her bag and jacket, waiting to see what would be said. This wasn't supposed to happen.

They'd gotten in their car, Daniel moaning about not seeing Rachel, when they'd caught sight of one of the men whose names he'd just tortured out of the guy. It had been too good of an opportunity to pass up. Parking the car, they'd dragged him down the darkened alley, and when things had gone too far, Daniel had used his gun rather than his fucking brains. Vincenzo should just kill him now, but then he'd have to explain what happened and he had no interest in drawing his bosses into this. They'd want to test her loyalty, and he had a feeling she didn't know enough about the mafia or the life to give a good judgment.

"What the fuck was she doing near the alley?" Daniel asked.

"Probably walking home, seeing as she was crossing the street, but you were too busy firing bullets to even care. How did you end up a soldier? Because right now, I'm not seeing any soldierly qualities in you."

"Fuck you, Vince. You don't know the first thing

of what I'm capable of."

"I know that you shoot your weapon like it's a fucking dick and don't care who gets hurt in the crossfire."

Daniel stood toe to toe with him. "You want to go there?"

"Gentlemen, I don't care what problem you have, but I need you to know and understand, you fight here, and this will be the last work I do." Doctor Alverez looked over at them. "Do I make myself clear?"

"Perfectly," Vince said. "How is she?"

"She's doing good, all things considered. Her heart and pulse rate are stable. I've removed the bullet and sealed the wound. She's going to need to take it easy. From her uniform I see she's a waitress. She's going to have to rest and relax." The doctor placed a large bandage across her wound.

Vince didn't like seeing her on the table, eyes closed, looking pale.

"I'll take care of her," Vince said.

"She's going to need to have this checked in two weeks."

"I'll bring her here."

"I'll come to you," the doctor said. "You never know who is watching, and I'd hate to be responsible for this young woman getting hurt." He removed his latex gloves. "Please, be careful, Vince."

He didn't need a warning, and he respected the doctor.

Men and women that were pulled into this world were often killed.

"Are you going to help me or do I need to take care of her myself?" he asked, looking at Daniel.

"I want you to remember this."

"Believe me, I'm not going to forget."

He paid the doctor the rest of his fee and lifted her up in his arms.

"Be careful. She'll hurt tomorrow," the doctor said.

Without a backward glance, he carried her to Daniel's car. Resting her in the back seat, he climbed into the passenger one beside Daniel.

"You shouldn't have done that."

"I didn't have much choice. You fucking shot her."

"Why couldn't you have just let her die?" Daniel asked. "What makes her so special? She's fucking plain, and an hour before you even met her, you were torturing the fuck out of another guy. See the problem I'm having here?"

"That guy deserved to die. This woman doesn't."

"Vince, I know you're a fucking weirdo and always have been, but even you can do better."

He clenched his hands into fists. "You mean the whores that often suck my dick."

"Yeah. One good thing about the Galiza family, they know how to take care of their own."

"Yes, and so they pick the ripest pussy to fuck. Haven't you ever wondered about how many men they'd had inside them? That as they're sucking your naked cock, their throats have already been covered in layer upon layer of sticky cum. A man's sticky cum. Let's face it, if you kiss one, you may as well be sucking a guy's dick."

Daniel looked pale. "Shit, man."

"When you go to these whorehouses, Daniel, many, many men have already been there. Their mouths, cunts, and asses are always on the menu. They're loose. They don't have anything tight anymore. Besides, I rather like the thought of the chase. When I don't have that need to chase, I use the whores." It had been a while since he used the Galiza whores though. He only ever went there when he didn't have time to find his pleasure elsewhere.

"You actually want the plain waitress?"

"She's not plain." He glanced into the back of the car. "I think she's stunning," he said.

"I don't … you know what, I don't even need to get it, okay? This is all my fault. I shouldn't have stopped at the diner."

"We did good tonight. One name is scrubbed off our list of enemies to kill. You should be happy about that."

"Fuck you, Vince. I don't need to hear this shit right now."

"I expect you'll keep your mouth shut about Arika."

"Who the fuck is Arika?"

"The waitress."

Daniel rubbed at his temple. "Yeah, I will."

"I mean it, Daniel. If something happens to her or a hit is ordered, I will hold you personally responsible for her and then I will come after you. Then you'll get to see what happens when I have a lot of fun and not just put on a show for you."

"I'm not going to tell. As soon as she's good though, you need to let her go. You don't want a weakness lying around for someone to come and pick up."

"Everything will be fine. I promise." He wasn't a fool. He'd not lasted this long because of his good looks.

No one ever got one past him. He was able to read people better than they knew themselves.

Daniel drove to his home and parked up. Vince had a nice place out in the suburbs away from any mafia family. If they wanted him, they called him. Galiza liked it that way. It gave him an added edge.

Lifting Arika into his arms, Vincenzo carried her through his home, going straight upstairs and placing her on his bed. He'd never brought a woman home.

The whores he fucked, he did so on their turf, never bringing them home to his sanctuary. This was the place he practiced, trained, and enjoyed reading. He didn't own a television nor was there internet here. He enjoyed music, that was all.

She looked so good on his bed though, her brown hair fanning out.

Pulling himself away, he made his way downstairs to find Daniel waiting with her bag and jacket.

"I'll see you tomorrow?" Daniel asked.

"Make it the day after."

"Vince?"

"Don't. I don't need to hear anything. I'm perfectly capable of doing what I need to do, thank you very much." He took the bag and jacket, then saw Daniel out. He held her jacket up to the light, and he saw the hole from the bullet. That would have to go.

Walking into the kitchen, he put the jacket on the counter. He'd burn it in due course. Opening her bag, he started to pull out books and her purse. Opening it up, he saw she had a couple of dollars and a few bits of change. Checking her ID, he saw her name was Arika Jane, just like on her name tag. It was a rather strange name, but he then pulled out his cell phone and dialed his private contact. Within half an hour, he had everything there was to know about the woman currently sleeping in his bed.

Her name, Arika Jane. The fact she was in the foster care system. No one knew her parents' identity so that made sense with the last name being Jane. She was in all senses a "Jane Doe," but they named her Arika. No family to speak of. She was twenty-one years of age, enrolled in college, taking classes in between working at the diner. She rented a small apartment that wasn't worth the money.

In all senses, she was a nothing and a nobody, until tonight.

Turning off his cell phone, he walked back upstairs and took a seat, looking at her.

For a plain woman, she really struck him hard. There was no way he could turn his back on her, especially not now.

She'd been an innocent, crossing the road, making her way home when Daniel's carelessness had hurt her.

This was all new for him. He didn't care for anyone.

What was it about this sweet little dove that he couldn't seem to shake?

****

Pain was everywhere.

Arika opened her eyes, staring up at the ceiling. Her side burned, and everything seemed a little fuzzy. Letting out a groan, she tried to roll over, but again, the pain was too intense.

Placing a hand on her stomach, she let out a scream as someone touched her hand.

"It's okay. You're fine. You've just got to take it easy."

She hadn't even realized that a light had come on and now she was staring at a man. The one from the diner. The one that kept looking at her.

"What's going on?"

He took her hand and pressed on her shoulders so she had no choice but to lie down.

"You don't remember?"

"Remember what?" she asked.

Like being struck, she remembered crossing the road, and the pain of being shot.

"You shot me."

"I didn't shoot you."

"I was shot."

"You were shot."

She glanced down at her body and saw she was only in her underwear.

"Where are my clothes?" she asked.

"I thought you'd be more comfortable without anything irritating your wound."

She took a deep breath. "I'm not at my apartment."

"No. You're in my bed."

"In your house?"

"Yes. You'd have to be in my house to be in my bed."

He sounded way too amused, and right now, she wasn't in the slightest bit.

"I got shot."

"You don't need to worry about that."

"I have to tell the police. Someone needs to know that there's a madman running around with a gun!"

"You don't need to tell anyone anything."

She shook her head. "I don't know what to do. I can't afford to be shot."

"You don't have to pay for anything. I had a friend take care of everything."

"Do I have all my organs?" she asked. Other than the pain from being shot, everything felt all right. She'd read an article in the paper a few weeks ago about organs being sold on the black market or something like that.

This couldn't be happening to her.

"You have all your organs," he said. "That's a rather strange question."

"Between getting shot and waking up naked here, I have a bit of a blank, and I'm trying to figure out what to do about that."

"You don't need to do anything about that."

"I've been shot."

"You keep saying that, but it's not really a big deal."

"Okay, I can't think right now." She pressed her hands to her face. "What do I do?"

"There's not a lot you can do. You'll stay here. Doctor's orders, you have to rest."

"I can't afford to rest. I have to go to work. I've got classes. My English assignment. I can't just sit around and be ... sick or in pain."

"You are in pain though. We seem to be going in circles over this matter. Getting stressed out is not good for you. You need to relax."

"I can't. I need the money." She winced at how greedy she sounded. "They'll find a replacement."

"If I promise that I can guarantee your job, will you please relax and take it easy?"

"You can do that?"

"There are a lot of things I could do. I'll only do them if you agree to my terms."

She didn't see the point in arguing with him. He'd won no matter what. "Fine. Fine." Dropping her arms down from her face, she turned her head to look at him. "You're not going to hurt me, are you?"

"No. I have no plans to."

"Good, because I don't want to die. Not yet."

"You have a plan of when you want to die?"

"I've got an idea, but there's so much I want to do before that day. I know it sounds crazy, and I can't believe I'm talking to you about this."

"It's fine."

She didn't think it was fine, not at all. "What's your name?" she asked.

"Vincenzo, but you can call me Vince. You're Arika."

"You remembered my name."

"I did."

She didn't know what to make of what was going on.

The rumors that filled the diner as she moved from table to table suddenly flashed through her head.

"You're part of the mafia?" She didn't seem to have any filter either. Slapping a hand to her mouth, she groaned as pain struck her again. Any sudden movement seemed to cause her pain. She hated that feeling. Nothing she did seemed to help.

Being helpless was something she wasn't accustomed to, and right now, she needed someone a lot. There's no way she'd be able to go into work like this.

She loved her job, even if it was long hours that hurt her feet.

"If you want to keep breathing, I suggest you keep those kinds of questions to yourself."

Gritting her teeth, she nodded her head, seeing the threat in his gaze. She didn't want to die.

"No questions. I get it."

"That's correct. It's better this way."

He wasn't apologizing. Watching him, Arika saw he wasn't used to making excuses for his life. This man was part of the mafia. No doubt about it and now her life could possibly be in danger.

From the frying pan into the fire.

"I won't tell anyone. I don't want to die." She spoke slowly, softly, hoping he didn't see her as any kind of threat.

"You shouldn't be worrying about this. What you need to do is rest." His gaze moved down her body.

She became more aware of her nakedness at his assessment of her.

Did he like what he saw?

Taking a deep breath, she looked at him, waiting.

"Are you in pain?" he asked.

"Yes."

"I'll be back."

She didn't move from where he'd put her.

The last thing she wanted to do was to give him any reason to be angry with her. She didn't do well with a person's anger.

Staring up at the ceiling, she admired his plain white walls. Not a crack in sight. On her bedroom ceiling there were three noticeable cracks. She'd gotten a ruler and measured them, which she did every single week to see if they were getting bigger. They weren't, but that didn't exactly give her any comfort.

Why was she thinking about her cracked ceiling when she was lying in a mafia man's bed?

This man was deadly.

Serious.

Scary.

He returned seconds later, holding a glass of water. "Here is the medication that the doctor gave. It should help you sleep and numb the pain for a little while."

She stared down at the pills.

"What is it?"

"They're painkillers, Arika. I have no reason to drug you. I don't do drugs."

He'd given her no reason to not trust him. Taking the pills and the water, she swallowed them down, thanking him.

"You're not used to having someone take care of you, are you?"

She shook her head, not really sure what to say.

"Do you take care of a lot of women?"

"No, you seem to be special to me."

She rolled her eyes, not believing a single word he said to her. They didn't know each other. Neither of them meant anything special to one another. He worked for the fucking mafia. There's no way she'd have anything to do with him. Her life was planned out. She didn't want, nor did she need, any complications.

"You're so easy to read," he said.

Turning to look at him, she found him smiling at her as if watching her amused him.

"I don't know what that means."

"You don't hide your feelings very well, do you, sweetheart?"

"I … this is all a little confusing for me. I don't know you. You're a killer for all I know."

He's mafia. Of course he's a killer.

She tried not to think about all the ways he could kill her without anyone finding her body.

He took her hand, at which she jolted from the contact.

"You're a real mystery. Does my touch repulse you?"

"I'm not used to stuff like this."

"Men touching you?"

"Anyone touching me, to be honest." She bit her lip. Why was she telling him all these things? He didn't own her heart or her mind.

He was a guy.

She didn't get along well with men.

This was crazy.

Maybe it was the medication he'd given her. She didn't know.

"You're a virgin?" he asked.

Her cheeks heated. "I don't want to keep on talking."

"It's fine. If it makes you feel better, I have a knack for making people talk."

"You do."

"Yes. It's why I'm so good at my job."

"What do you do?"

"I make people talk, spill their secrets, and I protect my bosses."

He's mafia.

He's a monster.

"I'm so tired."

"Sleep, sweetheart. Sleep."

Chapter Three

With the breakfast tray fully loaded, Vincenzo made his way upstairs to see his current guest. Not that he imagined she liked being called his guest. He'd watched her several times throughout the night try to make an escape, even though they had been pathetic attempts, seeing as she could barely move.

Clearly, it hadn't taken her very long to put two and two together to realize who he was, or at least who he was associated with.

Normally, he liked to see that fear that people often got when associated with him. Seeing the look in *her* eyes though had left him cold. Again, this woman was doing things to him that he wasn't entirely sure he liked.

This was all a new experience for him.

Opening the bedroom door, he saw she was missing.

Putting the tray on the bed, he glanced around the room. There was no sign of an open window. Just as he was about to check the rest of the house, he heard the toilet flush, followed by running water.

When she opened the bathroom door, she froze. "I just needed to use the bathroom."

"You're free to do so."

"But not free to leave."

"On doctor's orders, you must be taken care of."

"I, erm, I think I should be fine. You don't have to come and, you know, take care of me."

"Is it just me personally you have an aversion to?"

"An aversion to what?"

"Taking care of you?" He folded his arms, watching her.

She stood in her underwear with every single curve on display. She had a really nice set of tits, and he loved her hips. Damn, he could imagine holding them as he fucked her hard. She deserved a nice, good fucking. Something hard that made her scream.

Arika glanced down at her body and quickly started trying to hide herself.

"No need to do that for me."

"I'm … I've never been nude before in front of a guy." She slapped her hand to her mouth, and the jolt once again caused her to wince. "I really need to stop doing that."

"I brought you breakfast. I hope you're hungry."

As if on cue, her stomach rumbled.

"Sit. Eat."

"Do you always order everyone around?"

"Yes, and I always get what I want." He pulled back the covers, and she gently slid into bed. He couldn't help but stroke her skin as he placed the blanket back over her, making it look like an accident. She tensed up, but he ignored that.

Clearly a virgin when it comes to everything.

He put the tray on her lap.

"Now I want you to eat everything on this plate. It'll do you good."

She stared at the food, sucking her bottom lip between her teeth.

He wanted to pull it out and bite that lip. Have her mouth open so that he could taste her. She'd look so pretty with his dick sliding between her lips, hitting the back of her throat, swallowing him down. He'd make her take all of him as well, every single inch until he filled her mouth with his cum and watched her swallow every drop.

His dick hardened at the thought, and he quickly

adjusted himself so he wasn't in any kind of pain.

She poured some milk into the bowl of cereal he'd prepared for her. He had a lot of skills in the kitchen, but he didn't know what she liked just yet. Besides that, the way she kept fidgeting showed she didn't have an appetite.

"I'm not used to being taken care of," she said. "I've been alone for a long time. I can usually take care of myself."

"Well, you need someone now. I'll talk to your boss at the diner. Anyone else I need to speak to?"

"My college professor. Erm, I really need to finish a couple of assignments that I have."

"They're not in your bag?" He knew they weren't.

"They're at my place. I don't mind going home. You know. I can rest there."

"And I can see a lie when I'm being told one. You're not going home, not yet."

"I won't go to the cops."

"You don't need to go to the cops." She had her head bowed over her bowl of cereal. Reaching out, he gripped her chin. "You need to understand something here, Arika. You go to the cops, you die. Who I work for will kill you because you were at the wrong place at the wrong time."

"It doesn't exactly seem fair."

"Life isn't fair. Now, I will have a friend come here to take care of you while I go to your apartment."

"Who?" she asked.

"The man I was with last night."

He saw she wrinkled her nose.

"You don't like him? He has a thing for one of the waitresses that works there."

"I know him. It's why Rachel changed shifts. She

wants nothing to do with him. He kind of scares her."

"A lot of people in our line of work will do that." He couldn't help but smile as it was just so fucking funny. Daniel didn't have a clue that he was being avoided.

"Please don't tell him. Rachel was already scared about changing her shift. She doesn't want to get involved with him."

"If it helps I will talk to Daniel a little later and he'll stop bugging your friend."

She nodded.

"Eat your food. I'll grab you a shirt so you don't have to worry about covering yourself. I don't own a television, but I do have a vast collection of books."

"Any romance?"

"I can get you a few romance books if that's what you want."

"You can?"

"Yes."

"Have you read them?" she asked.

"That is not something I'm going to tell you."

He held out a shirt, and she pushed her arms in the air. He slid the fabric over her body, pleased with the fit. His clothes looked good on her.

Once she finished her breakfast, he took the tray and located the books he'd mentioned. He had read them as they were a nice way to relax after a long day of death and torture. Placing them on the bed, he called Daniel to arrange for him to keep an eye on her. With that done, he grabbed a bag to put her items inside, and within thirty minutes, Daniel was there.

"I can't believe you're making me babysit her."

"You've got no choice. If she is hurt or dead when I get back, I will keep you alive for a year while I make you pray for death. Do you understand me?"

"For fuck's sake, Vince. What is this? She's not even pretty."

"Do as I say, got it?"

"Got it. Not a hair will be harmed in protecting her."

"Good." He left his home, ignoring the suburban wives that were cleaning their cars. Most of them looked like they were being neglected by their husbands. He got a good kick out of watching the world go by. Seeing them flirt with either the postman or someone else that caught their attention. There was a young man who mowed lawns, and that kid had gotten a lot of personal attention.

He didn't need to be near the mafia to get his kicks. Just watching normal people was fucking crazy.

Climbing into his car, he headed toward the diner first. He had no doubt that one word from him and Arika would be clear to keep her job and have a few days' paid vacation. They didn't need to know that she had a gunshot wound that she was recovering from.

His cell phone rang, and he clicked the accept button, placing it against his ear. He had no problems driving past cops. They all knew his car, and if they didn't, running the plates would let them know who they were dealing with.

"Barbato," he said.

"Ah, my favorite executioner. What do I need to know?"

"I extracted the names of the traitors that would serve to throw off your crown and replace you. We took one out last night. It had to be a body dump as something came up. Don't worry, it also contains a message so those will know who they are dealing with."

"The Vitales need to learn to keep their own turf."

33

"They'll get the message."

"Is there anything else I need to know about?"

It was on the tip of his tongue to tell him about Arika. Galiza had been more than a friend; he'd been his savior. He didn't get along with all in the family seeing as Galiza had several sons who felt like their father showed him more attention.

There was no way he'd take over as a Galiza. He was merely a tool for their use, the mafia beast they needed to make the bad shit go away.

"There was a complication, but I'm dealing with it."

"Do I need to worry about this … complication?"

"No."

This was his safety net. He wasn't lying to Galiza. He was just not telling the man the whole truth.

"Then I will let you handle it the way you know how."

Conversation terminated.

Vincenzo hung up and continued with his plan.

****

The romance book had clearly been read, but that didn't mean Vincenzo had actually read it. Arika ran her fingers down the spine and wondered if he had. Would he have enjoyed this kind of book? He didn't seem like the kind of man who would read something like this.

Biting her lip, she flipped the book over, staring at the sexy man on the cover.

She liked a good romance.

For a few hours she could pretend to be like the heroine in the story, just waiting for that special someone to come and take her away. Of course, that would never happen, but she didn't need a man to be happy.

Movement near the door scared her. Holding the book tightly, she stared at the man from the diner last night, the same one that had been harassing Rachel. Well, not really harassing, but in a way, yes. She didn't know if asking for dates would constitute harassment. Rachel said most guys wouldn't be a problem, but, seeing as Daniel was who he said he was, she didn't want to get involved in that life.

"You're alive," he said.

Glancing down at herself, she nodded. "It certainly appears that way."

He tilted his head to the side. "I don't get what he sees in you. He barely knows you, and yet he's determined to keep you alive."

She didn't say anything as he walked into the room.

He shrugged. "Don't worry, I won't kill you. If you stay tense like that with a gunshot wound, you'll hurt later."

She tried not to tense, but, seeing as she was now alone with a man she didn't really know, she couldn't seem to help it.

He sat down in the chair near the bed.

Vincenzo had sat in it last night, watching her.

She didn't know if he'd even been able to sleep.

"Do you know who we are? What we're associated with?" he asked.

Staring at him, she nodded her head.

"Ah, so you know you're dealing with one of the deadliest messengers the mafia has?"

"You're a deadly messenger?"

"Not me. I'm the bodyguard to the messenger. Vince is…"

"Vince is the deadly messenger?"

"Yes. He has a knack for hurting people. For making them talk. For getting them to divulge all of their secrets, really. You know how it is?"

She shook her head. "I don't have a clue what you mean."

"Well the longer you stay here the higher the chance is that you're going to find out. I'd be careful around Vince. Nothing ever ends well with him."

"Why are you telling me this? Do you just want to scare me?"

"I want to prepare you."

"Prepare me for what?" She didn't like this man. He made her nervous.

"For what is to come if Vince doesn't get over this little obsession he's developed with you."

She stared at him, not really sure what to say.

It seemed in the past few hours she'd not been able to say anything of any real relevance in her mind. Between Vincenzo and Daniel, her life was in danger.

"He's part of the mafia, Arika, but he's not one of the most important families."

"He told me that if I knew too much it was dangerous for me. I don't want to know anymore." She didn't want to die.

"You're scared?"

"I just want to get well and go back to my life."

"Too late for that, I think. You're involved now. Whether you like it or not, you're not going to walk away. You see, Vince is someone special."

She noticed he kept calling the man who was taking care of her "Vince" and not his full name.

She rather preferred Vincenzo. It sounded less threatening to her.

"He's the one the mafia sends to get a message across."

She swallowed past the lump in her throat, seeing the joy in Daniel's face.

"You get off on scaring people?" she asked.

"I get off on doing my job. It's why I was placed with Vince in the first place. I keep him safe. Of course, that bastard is even more sick in the head than I am. I admire him. He's known as the 'Mafia's Beast.' He gets the job done. When he comes to call, there's going to be a lot of pain and a lot of death. He's got a reputation for torture. I've seen it with my own two eyes. I once saw him cut a man's dick off and shove it in his mouth. He then taped his mouth shut while he proceeded to cut another body part off him. It was a work of art, I tell you. Fucking disgusting, but so damn good to watch."

Tears filled her eyes.

She didn't want to be here, and this man was making it impossible for her to be comforted by what he was saying.

"This man will do whatever it takes to get the job done. Right now, you're a distraction. If I was you, I'd use whatever it is that has him so enthralled to keep him that way, otherwise it's not going to end well for you."

He leaned over, patting her leg.

She couldn't help but flinch at his touch.

The last thing she wanted was for him to touch her.

He laughed, the sound of delight spilling from his lips.

He got up and made his way toward the door.

He wants you to be afraid.

That fucker just got off on terrifying you.

Watching him leave, she saw the swagger in his walk, and she hated it. This man was a fucking bully. Thinking about Rachel, she didn't want to be another woman scared.

"How did he become this beast?" she asked.

She didn't really want to know, but she also didn't want to back down. This man got off on hurting people, scaring them.

Living in the foster system, she'd seen a lot of stuff. There wasn't a lot that could frighten her. Many of the kids would tell each other tales of some of the real shitty placements they'd been in. The abuse, the pain, the sex trades. All of it had been a living, breathing nightmare. It was why she stopped wanting to be adopted and just waited until she left the system when she was of age.

Daniel turned around.

For a second there was surprise on his face. "You want to know more?"

"Why not? You're more than willing to talk, and I'm a little bored." The last thing she wanted was for this man to think he'd won. There's no way she'd let that happen.

Fear wasn't something she was ever going to allow to defeat her.

He walked back to his seat and sat down. "You do surprise me."

"You think that's the scariest thing I've heard in my life?"

"I'm not talking about horror stories, girl. This is real life. Vince tortures people. Rips out their fingers, cuts body parts off, hurts them. He's even killed women too. Backstabbing whores that needed to be put in their place."

In the back of her mind, Arika actually gave a cheer for Rachel for changing her shifts. This man came across as the nice guy, but the reality was far worse than that. He was one of the biggest monsters out there.

"So he kills people. Tortures them. Does he use stuff?"

Daniel smiled. "That depends on the job, really. Whatever takes his fancy, he'll use on anyone. Knives, guns. I watched him shoot a guy in the leg, not to bleed out or have a quick death, that's not Vince's style. No, he likes to make it painful. The traitors always get what's coming to them."

"So, if it wasn't about bleeding out, what was it about?" she asked.

"He had a bunch of rats with him. Once he shot this guy and the scent of blood started to fill the air, so he unleashed the rodents and watched as they all swarmed around this guy. There was no way for him to escape. It was a thing of beauty, really. You'd be surprised what a group of thirty rats can do to a human."

She was going to be sick.

This was a really bad idea.

Up until last night she'd been in her own little bubble where no one could touch her. Now, she was living with a man who would be taking care of her. Only, the man taking care of her was a monster.

A monster she couldn't run from.

Did she know too much now?

Daniel kept on talking, and after a while each story seemed to bleed into another.

She had to get out of here.

Chapter Four

Vincenzo placed the bag of books on the kitchen counter, and within seconds Daniel was there.

"That didn't take long," Daniel said.

He noticed the smug look on his guard's face.

"I had a quick word with her boss and after that, I went to her apartment. I wasn't going to be long. You can leave now."

"You're not going to invite me to stay for dinner?"

"No." He poured himself a large glass of water and stared at Daniel. "You can leave."

"Wow, man, you're a real fucking charmer."

Daniel didn't linger though.

They were colleagues as well as friends, so Daniel knew when it was best to stay or go. If they weren't working together, they did hangout but Daniel was always chasing one pussy or another, and he wasn't interested in that.

Finishing off his water, he picked up the bag of books, along with the laptop that she'd need as well. He'd already gotten it disconnected from the internet, and he made his way upstairs to where Arika lay.

One look at her pale face and the fear that flashed in her eyes and he knew exactly what the fuck was going on.

"He told you some stuff," he said.

She held the blanket with a death grip as if that would save her.

"He told me a few things."

"About me?"

"Yes."

"I won't hurt you."

"But if your bosses give the order, you won't

have a choice, will you?"

"I'll have a choice. I'm not owned by them, Arika."

"They're the mafia."

"And I told you, the less you know the better."

He saw tears in her eyes, and he hated it.

"He wouldn't shut up. I didn't even ask at first."

"At first?"

"He got off on it. On me being afraid. I hated that. I didn't want to be afraid of him or what he was doing, but I was. So, when he went to leave, I wouldn't let him think that he had a way of scaring me. I asked him to tell me more."

Vincenzo took a seat, watching her. "He told you what I've done."

She nodded her head, the action jerky and scared.

"I've done a lot of bad things, Arika. In this line of work, you have to."

"Torturing men and women?"

"I needed answers," he said.

"But, what if they were innocent?"

"If they were innocent and there was proof they would be highly compensated."

"That kind of torture couldn't have been easy to live with after," she said.

"Yes, but more money and power are always a deal-breaker, Arika. The world is full of bad people."

"And you're one of those people."

"If I was to tell you that some of the men and women that I've killed had hurt children, the next generation of the mafia, what would you think?"

She went to speak, and he saw her pause. "In what way?"

"Forcing them to have sex with men or women they don't like. Hitting them, abusing them, exploiting them. I'm not saying the mafia is perfect, but the family I work fo0r, they don't believe in the exploitation of children, or in their torture."

"I don't want to talk about this anymore," she said.

"Some of the people I've hurt and even killed deserved it, Arika. I'm not going to make excuses for what I've done. This is who I am."

"It scares me."

"Do I scare you?"

She nodded her head.

"I've not done anything to harm you. I'm going to keep on protecting you because you are an innocent in all of this. You were merely at the wrong place at the wrong time. I won't hurt you. I will do everything to keep you safe."

He watched as she pushed a strand of hair out of her face, tucking it behind her ear. Holding up the bag he brought her, he smiled. "So I went through your apartment and found everything related to your course." He held up the laptop. "There is no internet service here."

"What about a deadline?"

"You'll print it out, or give me one of those USB drives, and I'll take it to your professor." He paused as she watched her. She was biting her lip. "I want to make one thing clear, Arika. If for whatever reason the cops come calling or questions start getting asked about you, I'll have no choice but to end your life, do you understand?"

He watched her swallow, the nerves clear on her face.

"I—"

He cut her off before she could say anything else. "I will do everything in my power to protect you. That means keeping you alive. I can only do that if you allow me to. Cops change things. It puts a hit on your head, and I will do it. Not only that, I will make it slow."

"I don't want to die."

"Then let's not send secret messages to your professor about where you are or what you've done. You want to stay alive and breathing so you can finish those plans." He saw the surprise in her eyes. "I saw the board you had, the plans you'd written on it. What you hope to achieve for the future. I found it a rather inspiring plan. You wish to help others."

Again, she nodded without saying a word.

"It's good what you're doing."

She looked at him. He saw the doubt in her eyes.

"I'm not really going to get far as a waitress though. There's so much I want to do with my life."

"We'll work together to help you achieve that." He took her hand, and at the first touch, she flinched. He didn't let her go though.

She stared at their hands, and after a second or two she gripped his firmly. It wasn't much but it was a start, and for now it meant he could trust her.

"Is this even allowed?"

"What?" he asked.

"You and me, talking together. Isn't the mafia supposed to be, like, an exclusive kind of thing?"

He smiled. Her question was so sweet.

"It's not an exclusive club, Arika. There are always people close to it that have nothing to do with it."

"Like?"

"Mistresses can be one."

"How? They must be pretty close to it."

"Some of the men take wives that are part of other families. They're often not good matches, and usually result in a great deal of unhappiness. So the men do what they must, and when they find the right woman, they take her as a mistress. Rarely does the life touch hers. She's there to provide entertainment. Some time away from their life."

He saw her thinking.

"But it does touch them."

He stared at her.

"You said rarely. That's not never. So, a mistress position must still be pretty dangerous."

"It is."

"I don't know how anyone could do that. Be part of a life. Especially with a married man."

"For the most part, the guy isn't really married. He must have heirs, obviously, but he wears a ring, that's it."

"I can't even believe you're telling me all this."

He didn't respond to that.

"What about the women?" she asked.

"The mistresses?"

"No, the wives. The women. Don't they get to have a little fun on the side?"

"No."

He saw her jerk back.

"Like that, just no?"

"It's not allowed in our life."

"Wow, talk about double standards."

"The wives don't need anything else. They're being taken care of. They've got sons. There's no need for anything else for them."

Her mouth dropped open in a perfect O of shock. He found that utterly cute. "You don't think she has a right to be with someone that ... I don't know, gets her hot and excited?"

Arika's cheeks were on fire.

"They don't need that."

"You're unbelievable. Women want that kind of stuff as well. Granted, not all women, but then not all men do either."

"They want sex?"

"Yes!"

"They get sex."

"Not with guys they actually want. They probably just have to lie there. I don't need to know anymore." She held the hand up that he wasn't holding and shook her head. "I can't bring myself right now to even think about this."

He chuckled.

"You're doing it to make me crazy."

"The women are not allowed to take lovers. If they do, it's in secret, and it's highly dangerous."

"Is that what you'd do? Marry who you're told and then expect her to live a lonely, miserable existence being your wife and only getting anything intimate when you deem it necessary to have sons?"

"I'm not part of the mafia like that. I'll not be providing anyone with sons that are needed. Whoever I take as my wife will be mine and, believe me, Arika, when she's in my bed, there won't be any need to take a lover. I'll make sure she's well-kept and gets everything her heart desires."

****

"You're a pretty good cook," Arika said, twirling her fork in the spaghetti.

"Living on your own, you learn these things. I've never been one for takeout food."

"Why were you at the diner then?" she asked, slurping up the spaghetti with the rich sauce he'd coated the pasta in.

She'd been in his home now for two days. During that time, the pain had started to lessen a little, which she loved. She'd also completed her assignment and caught up on her studying rather than reading a romance novel.

Fortunately, Vincenzo hadn't forced anyone to come and sit with her during this time to she didn't have to deal with any more scary stories. Daniel hadn't returned either, and it made her a little uncomfortable that she hoped he'd in some way ended that guy.

She wasn't normally a girl prone to violence, but she didn't like his friend. In the last couple of days, she'd learned a lot.

Not everything was about the mafia either. He worked for them, but he wouldn't go into their secrets and even though he spilled the beans on the mistresses, it wasn't exactly news either. They made films about the mafia, so she imagined a lot of stuff was there and easy to find.

"I was at the diner because of Daniel. It was late. I was hungry, and he picked the diner. I normally go in for an Italian place."

"Is that your favorite kind of food?" There was that little smile to his lips. She noticed he got that from time to time when she said certain stuff, and she wasn't sure why. Maybe it was the weird questions she asked.

This was the first time in her whole life when she'd been alone with a guy. Not only that, what else was she supposed to ask him?

"I love Italian. I do think it's the best food on the planet."

"I like Chinese," she said.

"No."

"Yes. Nothing you say is going to change that. They've got eggrolls. There, done," she said. "And shrimp toasts, which I love so much."

"Italian has meatballs."

"Meh."

"Seriously?" he asked.

"If that is all you've got to say then I can add noodles, rice, spareribs, I mean, come on, they've got wontons. They so beat Italian any day."

"Pizza."

She wrinkled her nose. "I've never really liked it. I mean, cheese, granted, but the bread part and everything else I don't like."

"I don't even know if I can let you live."

She burst out laughing.

In the two days they'd been together, she found herself growing less and less afraid of him. He wasn't someone to be scared of.

Vincenzo wasn't going to hurt her. He took care of her, running her baths, feeding her, checking her wound, redressing it, helping her.

He'd even taken her assignment to her professor and gotten the notes she would need in the two classes she'd already missed. If he was such a bad guy, he wouldn't have done that for her.

"You're the first person I know who doesn't like pizza."

"It's not like I grew up on it, you know. At the home where I stayed, pizza wasn't a luxury they could afford. We got food, but it always had to be stuff that helped to fill us up. Not something because it tasted good."

"I remember what that was like."

This made her pause with her fork to her lips. "You were in a foster home?"

He nodded.

"But I thought ... how can you have been in foster homes if you're part of the mafia?"

"I'm not one of their bastard sons, Arika. I told you. I work for them. The mafia did take me in and in a way I'm close with one of the families, but I came from the foster system. I was dumped on the orphanage's doorstep when I was nothing more than a baby, only a couple of days old they said. My birthday is unknown, so they gave me the date I was dumped instead. I was nearly a teenager before the mafia took me in."

"The same for me. No one knows anything about who I am or who left me." She shrugged. "I was there in a little car carrier. I didn't have anything else but the blanket the hospital wrapped me in."

"Didn't they check their records at the hospital?"

"They did, but they couldn't locate my parents. It looked like I wasn't even born there. That whoever had the blanket either worked there or had given birth there before or something. I'm not really sure. It's all kind of hazy."

"You never thought to look into it?"

"Getting a PI is a lot of money. I'm trying to build for my future. Besides, I wasn't good enough to want back then, and no one ever came back for me. So, I never even considered looking for them, seeing as they never came back for me and I never got adopted out. Why go hunting for someone that clearly didn't want you?"

"You're not upset by that?"

"In the beginning I was. Whenever a new family would come and I'd never even get looked at twice, I'd wonder why. You know. I'd be sad, and I'd cry for a little bit. Over time I didn't even bother trying. I didn't stand up as tall or smile or show the nice new family what a great person I was." She shrugged. "I concentrated on my studies as I knew one day I'd be out of there and I wouldn't have anyone but myself to rely on. So that's what I did."

"I was never adopted out either."

"You were taken by the mafia or a family within that group of people. You were adopted."

"My reputation preceded me. I had a thing about hurting … stuff. They heard about me, and the next thing I know, those skills I've been told to stop, they're wanting me to explore. Soon, I've got everything I ever wanted, and in time, I found my use for them. It wasn't for a family though, Arika. They didn't adopt me to let me be their son. I'm a means to an end."

"Doesn't that bother you?"

"No. I got out of foster care, and I make a very good living."

"I gathered that. You're living in the suburbs." She'd gotten out of bed this morning and looked outside to see the beautiful street where he lived. "Why do you live here?"

"It relaxes me. There's not a lot of danger here unless you don't mow your lawn on time."

"I did hear that the suburbs can be deadly."

He winked at her. "I'm the only deadly thing here."

She finished her food and didn't like the way his wink affected her. It wasn't a problem; of course it wasn't. He probably winked at a lot of women. What she didn't like was how good it felt to have him wink at her. Her stomach tightened, which caused a little pain, but she felt the wetness between her thighs.

She was attracted to him.

When had she stopped fearing him and now found him attractive?

"Considering you hate Italian, you made quick work of that."

"Your food is great."

"I will change your mind on your cuisine choice."

"If you could never have Italian again, what

would you do?"

"Quite simple, that's not an option."

She saw the seriousness on his face and couldn't help but chuckle, then wince. "You'd fight to always have your way?"

"Always. There's no such thing as living anyone else's way. I won't allow it." He leaned in close, and she got a scent of his cologne.

Again, the arousal hit her quite unexpectedly.

Leaning back, she tried to stay away from him. The shirt she wore was one of his, and his closeness didn't really help matters.

"I'll be up with dessert."

"I get dessert as well?"

"Every lady should have dessert."

When she was with him, he made her forget just how plain she was. She wasn't being a party pooper over this. Everyone she was with told her how plain she looked, how she needed to change to enhance what little beauty she had. One of the old waitresses at the diner said she should learn to be hot in the sack so then men would come crawling back for more.

She, personally, just wanted to be left alone.

However, Vincenzo made that quite impossible.

She enjoyed his company far more than she should.

Not only did she enjoy his company, but she looked forward to it as well.

He made her laugh, which she loved regardless of the pain. He made her smile and feel warmth where there wasn't any. There was a lot she liked about him, but she knew deep down, it couldn't last.

They were in different worlds, and even though for now theirs had collided, it didn't mean they'd work.

Chapter Five

A few days later Vincenzo watched as Arika walked slowly into the room. The wound in her abdomen was healing. The doctor had said it hadn't punctured any major organs or arteries as he'd been able to remove the bullet and stitch her back up. What he had warned about was the recovery time and the potential pain, seeing as it was in her abdomen and the muscles people used for simple things like walking, getting up and down, lifting cups, or books. Anything that required some strenuous activity would cause pain and would also prolong the recovery time.

She took things slowly.

He watched as she walked into the room and sat down on the sofa. She never came close to him unless he moved into her space. He wasn't sure if she was afraid of him or not. Several times when she'd looked at him, he was sure he caught a flash of desire, of need, reflected in her eyes. It would be gone as quickly as it appeared.

"I cannot believe you don't own a TV."

"I went into your apartment, remember. You don't own one."

"I don't need one."

"Neither do I."

"What do you do all day when you're on your downtime?"

"I sit in silence, read a book, work out."

"Where do you work out?"

"In my basement. I have a gym."

"It's not a special torture chamber?"

"Nope, I leave that to my bedroom." He winked at her, and her cheeks were red once again. "You've never been flirted with." It wasn't a question.

"Why are you asking me that?"

"I'm not. I'm stating it."

"We were talking about the television and your lack of one."

"You ever been stripped naked, kissed over every inch of your flesh? Had your legs spread open and someone lick your pussy?"

He saw her hands clench at her sides.

"Do we have to talk about this?"

"Why not? I want to talk about it."

"Just because you want to talk about it doesn't mean we should. I'm not comfortable with this."

"Then tell me why your nipples are hard as fucking pebbles pressing against the front of the shirt you're wearing."

She glanced down at her body. "I'm cold."

"It's a hot day. I've had to open a window."

"There's a draft?"

He smiled. "Come on, Arika. We're two people here."

"I've never been with a man. I wasn't lying to you when I admitted that. I've not had sex, ever."

"Not once?"

"No." She gritted her teeth as she spoke.

Her reactions to his questions were so cute. He would gladly sit and watch her all day.

"You've not been with a man, ever?"

"Do you like me to keep on repeating myself?"

"Yes."

"No. You're the first person to ever see me naked or to get me dressed. Just you."

"I rather like that." He moved from the far end of the sofa, close to her. Placing his finger against her hand, he stroked up and down.

She no longer flinched at his touch.

Instead, she looked down.

"You ever thought about what a man could do for you? How he could strip you naked, worship your body, fuck you until you forget your own name?"

"I've thought about it a lot. Doesn't mean it's going to happen, so there's no point in thinking about it." She pulled her hand away

He could push the issue, but instead, he rested his head back against the sofa, closing his eyes.

"Do you ever think of taking a woman hard?"

This got his attention.

Lifting his head, he saw her looking at him. The fire in her eyes caught him completely off guard.

"I *have* taken women hard."

She licked her lips, looking past his shoulder. "You've had women on their knees before you, lips open, forcing them to take your cock to the back of their throat until they gag. Holding their hair in your grip so they know who has control and who doesn't." She tilted her head to the side, and he didn't know how she could look so innocent with the words spilling from her lips.

"I've done that."

Her gaze came back to his.

"I've also had it where I've kept hold of their hair and forced them to take my cock even though I'm too big. I need a woman to be soaking wet, otherwise there is always a bite of pain when I fuck them. When I thrust inside that first time, if they're not dripping then they feel every single inch of me. The tighter the cunt, the more pain." He leaned in close, liking the game they were playing. "You know what else I love?"

She didn't pull away. "What?"

"I love when they scream my name, beg for more, and I smack their ass, leaving my mark for them to see when they look in the mirror. There's nothing better than leaving a brand on their skin."

He was sure he caught a moan from her lips.

"I'm thirsty. Want a drink?"

"Love one."

He got off the sofa and walked into his kitchen. His dick was rock-hard, and all he could think about was wrapping her long brown hair around his fist, forcing her to open her lips to take him. If she didn't do a good job, he'd smack her ass, letting her know he wasn't happy with the mediocre job she'd done.

She's a virgin.

There was no doubt in his mind that she was a virgin, completely untouched, but that didn't mean she wasn't needy. That she didn't imagine his cock filling every single one of her holes, or that she craved that kind of attention.

She'd never been wanted before.

No one paid her any attention.

Even Daniel had said there was no appeal to her, that he considered her way too plain to even look at twice.

Vincenzo didn't think of her as plain.

Far from it.

He thought she was a beautiful woman, through and through. She wasn't beautiful in the sense that she'd turn heads to look at. There's no way he'd even pretend that she was. No, to him, she held something in her eyes. In the way she walked.

Her life hadn't been easy, but rather than roll over and die, she'd forced herself to get back up. To keep on fighting. To do whatever it took to live another day.

Filling a kettle with water, he placed it on the stove.

Gripping the edge of the counter, he could imagine her on her knees, waiting for him, her pussy wet.

There was something in her eyes, a power at

times she didn't know she possessed.

What would it be like to take a virgin, to give her everything? To show her what she'd been missing? Her first time wouldn't be some fumbling in the back of a car by some teenage boy only interested in getting his dick wet.

Arika wasn't like other women.

She had a power that she didn't even realize that she had. He saw it every single time he looked at her.

Maybe it was just him that saw it though.

There was so much he could do with her, show her.

She'd gotten over her fear of him, and in turn, he'd come to trust her. It had only been a few days, but her need to survive helped their situation a whole lot.

He made them both a cup of coffee, and once his dick was under control, he walked back into the room.

She sat in the same place, head back on the sofa, looking so calm. Her hands rested on her thighs. The shorts she wore showed her pale skin that hadn't been touched by the sun.

The rest was doing her good as well.

He noticed she smiled a lot more, and there didn't seem to be that worry or stress in her gaze.

Her boss had wanted to fire her, had even said that he wouldn't pay for a waitress that wasn't there. Vincenzo had paid him well to not only keep her on, but to also pay her while she wasn't turning up, with a hefty amount for the boss himself. He always got what he wanted, and if money hadn't done the trick, next would have been a whole lot of violence.

As a kid, he'd been prone to pain and torture before considering other methods. Getting older, he took different approaches depending on the person.

"Thank you," she said, taking the cup from him.

There was a pinch to her lips as she held it but nothing like it was when she first arrived.

"You're a handy man to have around," she said. "Cook, clean, make drinks."

"I've lived alone for a long time. You learn these skills as you go."

She chuckled. "You wouldn't pay to have someone come and clean or fix your meals?"

"No. I like doing stuff by myself. I've enjoyed your company a lot the past few days, Arika."

"Thank you. I rather like being with you too."

****

"I won't bite, you know. There's no dungeon down here," Vincenzo said.

Arika rolled her eyes. "I'm not worried about that. These steps seem kind of steep, and I'm, you know, not wanting to hurt myself more."

The pain with moving had been getting less every passing day. She didn't know how long she'd been with him as she lost count, each day blending into the other, and the truth was, she didn't want their time to end.

With no pain, it meant she'd be going home.

She couldn't even believe that she was sad about that. Vincenzo wasn't always home. He still went out and had a job to do. There were times he returned in different clothes, and she knew without a doubt he'd been doing something bad. She never asked about it though. Did that make her a bad person because she didn't want to know? It's not like knowing would do anything different. She couldn't change what he did or who he did it to.

He never brought it home.

She winced.

There it was again. When did she start thinking of this place as home? This was not her home. She'd have to go back to her apartment soon.

Rent was due.

She had to go to work.

Vincenzo would be a thing of the past.

Gripping the railing, she started down into the basement. She didn't want to sit on her own upstairs while he worked out, so she'd asked if she could come and sit with him.

She liked being in his company ... a lot.

With each step she took down to his basement, she saw more of his home gym. There was lots of equipment, from weights to running machines. In the far corner she saw a mannequin set up with points on it, and knives lined up on the walls. Clearly target practice.

The gym screamed danger, violence, and control.

"Take a seat."

"You're not going to make me work out."

"Not in your condition."

She nibbled her lip, feeling guilty. "About that, I need to tell you something."

"It's not hurting as much for you to get around."

She took a seat in the corner, watching as he stretched out on the mat. His clothes were skin-tight. His muscles seemed to bulge, and they looked so tempting, so hot, so sexy. She couldn't look away as he held his arm across his body, then the other way. He bent down, touching his toes, and then he grabbed a skipping rope. Who could have thought that a man jumping up and down, never once missing a beat, could be sexy?

The control.

The energy.

Just every single part of him turned her on. With him counting, she glanced down his body, and with the clothes being really tight, she caught sight of his ... bulge.

What was happening to her? Since coming to

know him, she'd found herself more and more obsessed with sex.

It wasn't like she wasn't aware of desire and needs and wants. She had them. There was no denying her own needs, but this was more than that. Between work, school, and just living life, she'd never given it much thought. The only time she allowed herself to think about those kinds of possibilities were in the few moments before sleep took her. When her body seemed to want something.

Vincenzo was a large man.

There were times she imagined his arms around her, holding her in place as he took her. More than anything she wanted to know what it would be like to have him between her legs, taking her, wanting her, showing her exactly what it was like to be a woman.

Pushing those thoughts aside, she focused on his words.

"Yeah, it's not taking me as long. The pain is minimal. I'll be able to go back to work. You know, get on my own two feet again."

"I already figured that." He put the skipping rope down, and she watched him sit back on a bench that had weights above him and start to push them up into the air.

His arms thickened, veins popping out.

He looked so fucking hot.

"Would you like me to walk home?"

"I'll take you back to your place, Arika. You don't need to worry about that. You're not ready yet, but in a day or so, you'll be fit and ready to go back home."

She didn't like that but didn't say anything. Pushing some hair behind her ear, she watched him continue to pump up the weights. After she counted to twenty, he placed them back on the pole above him.

He got up and added more weights, then did

exactly the same.

After he'd done that, he moved toward the running machine. He didn't hold onto the bars. He clicked in whatever he needed and the conveyor belt thingy started moving, and he ran.

She watched his feet then his body as moved.

He wasn't going anywhere, but watching him turned her on.

As she pressed her hands together, he stayed running for about ten minutes. He moved to a bench, sat down, and lifted up some large barbells, his elbow resting on his thigh as he pulled them up.

"You do this regularly."

"I've got no choice. I have to be at the peak of fitness."

"No room for error."

"Exactly."

"Do you go to a shooting range as well?" she asked.

He looked up at her. "Not for a long time. I no longer need practice. My aim is impeccable."

Pressing her thighs together, she watched him change arms and repeat the exercise. Again, his routine wasn't over as he picked up a set of knives and stood back. She watched as he threw them, hitting every single cross on the mannequin.

"You ever thrown them at a person before?" she asked.

"Yes, and moving targets. I'm a good shot."

"That thing's not alive so it doesn't really count."

"Want to stand in?"

"Excuse me?"

"Stand in place of the mannequin. I won't hit you, I promise."

"No, that's fine."

"You don't trust me."

"Trust is earned."

"You're still breathing."

"I got shot."

"Not by me. Come on, Arika. Live on the dangerous side."

"This is crazy." Even as she said it she got to her feet and made her way over to the wall.

Hands clenched into fists, she stood perfectly still, staring at him.

"You can't move."

"Believe me, I won't."

"Or flinch."

She gritted her teeth. Flinching wasn't something she could guarantee.

"You know what, this is crazy. I shouldn't do this."

He threw a knife, and she gasped.

She'd felt it as it passed over her, the air whooshing the fine hairs on her arms.

"Don't look so impressed," he said. "You still want to move?"

She didn't budge.

He threw another knife, this time going past the opposite arm and landing far from her.

"You know, none of these are hitting a target," she said.

Vincenzo chuckled. "The point of them is to not hit a target, Arika. You don't want me to actually get you, do you?"

She stared at him as he threw another knife. He wouldn't hit her.

With each knife that he threw, she felt herself trusting him more and more.

He could have left her for dead.

According to Daniel, he should have.

He hadn't killed her.

Vincenzo had done everything he could to keep her alive. On the last knife, he threw it and it went between her thighs.

She stood still as he walked up to her. His body seemed tense.

When he was close, she had no choice but to tilt her head back to look at him. He was something else.

Her tits felt heavy, and her pussy pulsed. She wanted him more than anything else.

"I don't know what I've got to do to prove to you that I'll protect you, Arika. I will never, ever hurt you."

He bent down, and she watched his hand reach the floor between her thighs and pick up a knife. He held it up for her to see.

Tucking some hair behind her ear, she nodded. "I'll just go and sit."

On shaky legs, she went back to her corner and waited as he picked up the knives. He continued to do his workout routine while she watched and waited for him to finish.

Nothing can come of this.

In a few days you'll be home and he'll forget about you.

She hated the shot of pain that struck her at knowing she wouldn't be seeing him again. That he was going to move on and it wouldn't be with her.

Get over yourself.

He's a monster.

A killer.

Trained to hurt traitors.

Then why did she hope that one day she'd see him again?

Chapter Six

The doctor had given Arika the all-clear, which was why Vincenzo was standing in her apartment watching her. Her bag was on the main coffee table, and he hated that she looked a little lost. The clothes she wore were the ones he'd given her.

She glanced around the space that made up her apartment. It didn't even begin to compare to his suburban life.

"You really didn't have to follow me up here. I can take care of myself."

"Says the girl that got shot."

"I wouldn't have been shot if your partner knew what he was doing and had much better aim."

"I'll be sure to remind him of that."

"That would be good."

"In the meantime, don't go near any open alleyways. Just avoid them."

"I'll do that. Not too keen on alleyways anyway. Will I see you again?" she asked.

She wasn't looking at him, and he watched her.

They were both prolonging this meeting, and that wasn't good for either of them. This wouldn't ever work. She wasn't fit to be in his world.

"No, that's not going to happen."

"You're not going to stop by the diner."

"No."

"Oh."

"It's better this way."

"That's fine. I understand. You've done more than enough to help me. I get it."

"I doubt that you even know what you're talking about."

"That's kind of rude." She stared at the floor.

She composed herself and then smiled at him.

It didn't quite reach her eyes, and he hated himself for hurting her, but there was no other way.

"Thank you for everything you've done for me. I know you didn't have to."

She held her hand out, and he shook it.

She had a firm grip but not too hard.

"I'll also make sure you don't see Daniel either."

"You'll keep him away from the diner?"

"I'll be sure to try. I can't guarantee anything." He winked at her. "Have a good life, Arika Jane." With that, he walked out.

Didn't look back.

There was no point in looking back.

They had no business being together.

Even when he walked out into the street, he didn't look up, even though he'd be able to see her window. He knew she was watching.

Climbing into his car, he took off, heading toward one of the family homes where Daniel had already told him to be.

Driving in that direction, he let his windows down and just let the ride clear his head. Right now, he didn't want to think. Life went on, and as much as he didn't want her to go home, he couldn't bring himself to force her to be part of this life. While she'd been staying in his home, he'd seen another side of this life.

They'd been talking about mistresses, and one of Galiza's mistresses had been caught trying to sell family secrets. She thought because he hadn't been around to visit her, that he was going to replace her. Out of jealousy and spite, she'd tried to bring him down, and in doing so, she'd been made an example of.

She'd gone to the cops, turning rat on them.

The entire incident had left a bad taste in his

mouth.

Galiza hadn't allowed him to deal with her.

He had to watch his boss in action. It didn't start with an easy kind of torture. No, that would have been way too quick. First Galiza had made his men use her. Take her body, fuck her until she had no doubt that she was nothing but a useless whore. A cum bucket, as he said. There had been so many men, and Vincenzo had no choice but to watch. At first, she'd tried to enjoy it, but then the torture had begun.

Her body was cut, slashed, burned, and the scent of burning flesh and the sounds of screams filled the air.

This was what they did to traitorous whores. By the time she drew her last breath, she'd been reduced to nothing.

She'd pissed and shit herself, begged and pleaded until Galiza finally got what he wanted. Whatever sick and twisted satisfaction he got from the episode.

In doing so, it had reminded Vincenzo exactly why Arika couldn't be his.

She deserved a life away from all of that. There's no way in hell that he'd ever allow anything like that to touch her. To get near her. So, he'd walked away, and now she was free to live her life. To be with someone who deserved her.

Not someone who was going to spend the rest of his life killing the people he was told to do.

Pulling up at the mansion of Galiza, he saw Daniel leaning against his car, smoking a cigarette.

He'd seen Galiza torture many women. Some were slow; others were quick. Normally, it didn't affect him. With Arika in his life, it had.

"Do we know what this is about?" he asked, walking over to Daniel.

"I'm guessing it has to do with this Vitale

bullshit. Cops are riding a few of the businesses. The strip clubs and massage places. We had a raid on one of the strip clubs. Couple of the bitches are in custody. The lawyer's on the case, but it doesn't take away the fact that they know stuff because of his last mistress spilling shit to them."

They were not allowed to use her name.

"We better go in then."

"You deal with *her*?"

"She's dealt with. Don't bring her up again and don't go back to that diner."

"I want to go and see that chick."

"You don't see that chick. There will be others out there like Rachel. She's nothing. I promised her that you'd keep your distance. We dealt with your fuck-up. Now let her go."

"You should have left her fucking ass in the street to die."

"And if she didn't die? They go to the diner, look over security footage, see who was last in her section. Grow the fuck up, Daniel. I was doing everything I could to keep us from getting locked up."

"No, you were thinking with your dick, but if you like to think otherwise, be my guest."

"Are we going to have a problem here?"

"No problem. Just don't tell me who to look for."

"I'll keep you alive for every single week you don't go there."

"I'm already alive," Daniel said.

"Because I haven't grown bored with you yet. Try me, Daniel, we'll see."

"So, the great mafia beast has a weakness. I didn't see that shit coming." Daniel smirked, slapping his chest. "Keep your panties on, buddy. I have no interest in the diner anymore. Found something more entertaining.

Shall we?"

He didn't say anything as they made their way inside Galiza's home.

The women were nowhere to be found, so they were probably in the kitchen, far away from any of this mess.

Taking a seat down from Galiza's sons, Vincenzo sipped at the water that was on the table. He did this every single time to show he wasn't afraid. There were tales of poison being put in the drinks, and everyone for a time had been afraid of that. Galiza himself told Vincenzo he'd started the rumor. No one got near their water to poison them.

Daniel was near the other soldiers. His rank was not as high as Vincenzo's.

Sitting back, he watched Galiza's sons. None of them were paying attention to the others. He didn't trust any of them, and they certainly didn't like him.

Finally, after five minutes, the man himself came out. Galiza. He took a seat at the table, nodding at all of them.

"Thank you all for coming. I imagine you've all got better shit to be doing. We've had a series of raids and police interventions on several of our businesses."

Vincenzo listened to each point that he already knew. Business being ruined. Their affairs being looked into and they had also had a shipment of coke that had been seized by cops, which they were working on removing all connections to themselves.

"So, the first order of business, I need the cops that whore spoke to. I want to know everything about them. Who their families are, the precinct they work for. We can either end this with civility or they can swim with the fucking fishes, as cliché as that shit sounds. Got it? I want you handling that, Barbato," Galiza said, looking at Vincenzo.

"Consider it done."

He listened as Galiza handed jobs down to each man. All of them were given a job that was either Vitale detail or handling of the businesses that had been targeted.

"I want to hear noise about this. I want the streets to know that we don't sit down and take betrayal easily. I want blood. I want everyone to get the fucking message."

With that, they were all ready to go.

He had a job to do first, and that meant getting his hands fucking dirty. Cops were always difficult to handle, especially if they had nothing to lose.

****

One month later

"Come on, it'll be fun," Rachel said.

"Going out on a blind date does not sound like fun." Arika grabbed the two plates of loaded burgers with extra fries before turning to her friend. "Believe me, I've done the whole blind date thing. He doesn't show." She'd tried it once at the last place she worked. It turned out the guy had arrived, taken one look at her, and left without giving her any warning.

She of course was left waiting, wondering what the hell to do.

"This is not a blind date though. This is a bunch of people, girls and guys, getting together Friday night at a bar. There's dancing, booze, and later we'll go out for food. Come on, Arika. You've got to live a little. You know. What happened to you during that break?"

"Nothing."

She left the kitchen, and Rachel stood back so she could serve two construction workers their food. They were diner regulars. She smiled as they thanked her before tucking in. The diner wasn't so busy tonight, but she didn't mind the easy shift. The couple of weeks she had off due to illness that no one could know about, she caught up on a lot of studying, work, and she finally had her life in order. For the past month she'd been panicking in case a bill landed in her mail, but as yet, nothing.

Heading over to the coffee machine, she filled up her pitcher, and Rachel was there.

"Are you going to tell me what you did on that vacation? I've heard a couple of girls talk and they said a guy with a suit came in. He had a meeting with Frank and then ta-da, you still have a job."

"It's nothing. Honestly, I just needed some rest. What will it take for you to stop asking so many questions?"

"So easy. Come out with us Friday night. Come on, Arika. It'll be fun. I know you do believe in having fun, right?"

"I don't know."

"Stop being a party pooper."

"I'm not being a party pooper."

"Then come to the club. Prove to me you know how to have a good time." Rachel started shaking her chest and shimmying from side to side. "Come on, Arika. Show me how to have fun."

"Fine. Fine. Just stop rubbing your body all over me."

"Honey, you so need to get laid if you think for even a second that is me rubbing my body all over you."

Arika didn't want to think about sex or anything to do with men. Since *he'd* left her in her apartment alone, something had been completely wrong with her. Most nights were spent yearning for him and his touch, and she just couldn't shove aside the need building in her head. Her fantasies were filled with him.

"Can we not talk about that? Okay."

Rachel hugged her close. "Wear something sexy. A dress that's low-cut. You've got to show off those babies. They are so fucking sexy to see." Rachel kissed her cheek.

It was that nagging conversation three days ago that had Arika standing at a bar, wearing a black cocktail dress that molded to every single curve, low-cut as Rachel asked. She watched as Rachel stood in the center of the crowd, all of them cheering as she downed another shot.

Arika had ordered a beer and was carefully sipping the light lager.

She and alcohol didn't mix well. The men were hanging on to Rachel's every word. Each time her friend turned toward her, she'd tip her beer bottle at her friend and force a smile to her lips.

This was why she didn't want to come.

She seemed like an outsider looking in. She wouldn't feel sorry for herself tonight, and at least while she was out at a bar, she refused to think about *him*.

The guy that had shot his way into her world, literally, had blown her mind, and left her high and dry. Not that she blamed him.

The man was dangerous with a capital D.

"Come on, honey, I didn't mean to leave you sitting here all on your own," Rachel said, grabbing her arm.

"Don't worry."

"We're having fun. Come on, let's dance."

Before she knew what was happening, she was on the dance floor. Rachel let out a whoop as a long, upbeat number came on. Arika didn't recognize it, and copying her friend's moves, she tried to dance along.

By the time the song ended they were both laughing, but Rachel wasn't ready to leave the dance floor.

"Have you seen anyone you want to leave with tonight?" Rachel asked.

"Nope."

"You've got to have seen someone."

"I'm just enjoying dancing and being away from everything." She grabbed Rachel's hands and whooped. "Come on, stop worrying so much about everything."

They danced together, and as she anticipated, two guys moved between them and Arika let them, especially as Rachel looked more than happy to be part of that sandwich.

Leaving the dance floor, she stood in line for the toilet, waiting her turn. Pushing some of her hair off her face, she folded her arms across her chest, trying to keep her composure. She wasn't one for wasting her time in nightclubs. She should be at home studying even though she'd done as much studying as anyone could do. The line didn't take that long to diminish, and she was in and done within minutes. She left the bathroom and came to a stop as she bumped into a very hard masculine chest.

She recognized the scent of him immediately.

Her body tensed up, and as she looked up, she saw him. Vincenzo.

"Arika," he said.

Just the sound of her name coming from his lips made her ache for more.

"Vincenzo." She glanced around, seeing no one. "I ... what are you doing here?"

"This is a nightclub for people to have some fun."

"You're here on a date."

"Not on a date."

"Oh."

"You?"

"No date. My friend from work wanted me to

come. She kept nagging me, and I finally caved."

"You're not having fun?"

"It's not really my scene."

"What about dancing?" he asked.

She couldn't believe they were discussing dancing.

"My dance partner was stolen."

"Then he wasn't a good partner."

"Oh, it wasn't a he, more of a she." She shrugged. "So, how have you been?"

"Busy."

"Right, I better go."

She really didn't want to.

As she made to move past him though, he caught her arm. "Want to dance with me?"

She should pull out of his arms, shake her head, and tell him no.

She didn't.

"I'd love to dance."

He slid his hand down, taking hold of hers and leading her onto the dance floor. Biting her lip, she tried not to show how fucking happy she was about this. She spotted Rachel dancing with the two men she left her with.

Ignoring the fast beat of the music, Vincenzo took control, drawing her close to him. One of his hands was at her waist, the other near the base of her back.

"Why did you come to this nightclub?"

"Is this one owned by your bosses?" she asked.

"Just answer the questions, Arika."

"Rachel picked it. She said it was a good one and that it was a lot of fun. I didn't think about who owned it or anything like that. Should I leave?"

"Not yet."

"If it's so dangerous for us both to be seen

together, why are you dancing with me right now?"

"Because, you're just a woman in a bar and I'm just a man waiting to get laid."

She looked up at him.

He wasn't looking around the club but focused on her.

"No one will ever know who you are. We can have women that are a one-time-only deal."

"Ah, the double standards."

"Have you thought about me, Arika?"

She loved and hated it when he said her name. It made her a little weak.

"Have you thought about me?" she asked.

"I asked you first."

"Do you always get what you want?"

"Most of the time."

"That must be nice."

"It has its benefits. Of course, it makes me very spoiled."

She didn't see a point in lying to him. "Yes, I thought about you. A lot."

"At this very moment, Arika, we're two people in a bar. We have no past, no future."

"Okay."

"So, what I want to know is if you're willing to come to my apartment within the city a few blocks from here and have yourself completely and totally fucked by me."

She had stopped dancing.

"You can say no," he said.

"You want to sleep with me?"

"No. I want to take that cherry, Arika. I want to give you a night you'll never forget. I want to fuck your mouth, your pussy, and if at all possible, fuck your ass. I want to consume you, and tonight I will do that."

"For one night?"

"For one night. There will be no repeat performance."

"For my safety?"

"Yes. It's your decision. I will respect it."

Staring at him, she knew there was no way she'd say no. She wanted this. She wanted him.

"I've just got to say goodnight to my friend."

Chapter Seven

Waiting to take Arika home was sheer fucking torture. Vincenzo was used to waiting though. He'd been at the nightclub after a hard day's work to have a drink and unwind. He'd been in the VIP section that overlooked the dance floor when he caught sight of her. He'd seen her drinking alone at the bar, then move onto the dance floor with her friend before leaving to go to the bathrooms. He should have stayed away, but this was his one chance.

For the past month he'd done everything that Galiza had needed. He'd found the cops responsible, both of them partners with families. All it had taken was showing up on the right day for them to agree to hand over the evidence and point the case elsewhere. The Vitales were being handled, but that would always be an ongoing problem that wouldn't end overnight.

He'd just gotten done sending a message to a pimp who thought he could use Galiza streets to sell his whores, and the last person he'd expected to see was the woman that plagued his thoughts.

Daniel hadn't brought her up again, and keeping to his promise, Vincenzo had not stepped foot inside her diner or near her apartment block.

Seeing her alone though, it was too good of an opportunity to miss.

With the elevator doors pinging open, he saw she was nervous, but he also saw her arousal. Her nipples were tight and hard, pressing against the front of her dress. If she'd been living with him, there's no way he'd have let her out that night. He'd have shown her what he'd like to do to her body.

Opening up his apartment door, neither of them spoke as she stepped over the threshold. Closing it, he grabbed her arm and pressed her up against the door, trapping her between his body and the door. Before she could form any kind of protest, he held her hands above her head, and with the other, he teased a finger down the front of her dress. "Did you wear this with the intention of getting fucked?"

"Rachel told me to wear something nice. Something that would show off my boobs."

"Do you do everything you're told?"

"Not always."

Teasing a finger over the dress, he stroked her nipple, moving between the valley and showing her other nipple equal attention. It wasn't enough. He wanted more, couldn't get enough of her. Releasing her hands, he spun her around so that her back was facing him and her front was pressed against the door.

Within seconds, he had her zipper down and her dress at her waist. Holding onto her hips, he pressed a kiss to her shoulder.

"I've never done anything like this before."

Pushing his cock against her ass, he tugged her hair over one shoulder, biting her neck right over her pulse. "I know, and it turns me on to know that my cock is going to be the first one inside your tight cunt, baby. You want it, don't you?"

"Yes."

She spoke the word so softly that he nearly didn't hear it.

He shoved the dress past her generous hips and watched it spill to the floor at her feet. Running his hands down over her ass, he groaned at seeing the thong that she wore. "Now this is sexy."

He spread the cheeks of her ass and watched the piece of fabric that lay against her anus. Moving his hands down between her thighs, he cupped her pussy.

She moaned as he felt the wetness of her thong. Sliding a finger beneath the fabric, he teased between her slit, touching her clit then down near her entrance. With his other hand, he flicked the catch of her bra and helped her to remove it.

"I won't go easy on you tonight, Arika. I want to fuck and do it hard. I don't want to be gentle. I'll make it good for you though, I promise."

Removing his fingers, he spun her around and stared into her brown eyes. She didn't look worried or nervous.

He saw the excitement in her gaze. She wanted this as much as he did, maybe even a little more.

As he stared at her, he removed his jacket, letting it fall to the floor, followed by his shirt. Kicking off his shoes, he shoved his pants down to the floor until he was standing before her naked.

His cock was rock-hard, the tip leaking copious amounts of pre-cum which he rubbed into his length, showing her what she could have.

"You want this, baby?" he asked.

She nodded, and he took her hand, wrapping it around his dick.

"While you're here, you're going to use words and you get to have everything your heart desires." He gripped her ass. "Because I intend to have you every single way I've been imagining for fucking weeks now." He slapped her ass, making her yelp. The sound echoed around the room.

"Please," she said, touching him.

He grabbed the straps of her thong and tugged, snapping it from her body. Tossing it on the floor, he shoved her hand away and lifted her up in his arms with ease. Carrying her through to his bedroom, he dropped her on the bed.

This room was built for sex. He'd made it that way.

Every single wall possessed a mirror. When he fucked, he liked to see everything. Seeing a woman come apart was a favorite pastime of his. But he also got off on some seriously kinky shit as well. Forcing a woman to see her true need. Some of the women he'd bedded hadn't been able to watch themselves. By the time he'd been through with them, they didn't have a choice.

"On your knees. Up here. Look at me." He had her staring into his eyes.

She didn't back down, her hands resting on his chest, running up to grab his shoulders.

Cupping her face, he tilted her head back, and slammed his lips down on hers. The instant their lips touched, she gasped, and he took full advantage, plunging his tongue inside.

She wasn't used to having a man touch or kiss her.

He didn't mind her inexperience though. He fucking loved it, knowing no other man had touched her, had wanted her. They didn't know what they were missing. The passion brimming beneath the surface was right there. All a guy had to do was look hard enough to find it. He'd spotted it that night in the diner.

Now he had her in his arms, for one night.

It could only be one night as well.

He wouldn't risk her life, not for more.

She cupped his face before sliding her hands into his hair, holding him tightly as he continued to ravish her mouth.

By the time he broke the kiss, her lips were red, swollen, and well-kissed. Moving his hands down her body, he cupped her tits. They were as good as he imagined they would be, huge tits with nice, tight red nipples, begging to be sucked. He took one into his mouth, and he stroked his thumb across the hardened bud of the other.

She pressed her thighs together, and he knew in that moment that her tits were sensitive. He moved to her other nipple, giving her the same kind of attention. He could gladly spend all night sucking on those beauties, but his dick was getting harder and he wanted her to be ready.

He had no intention of being soft on her, so her pussy was going to have to be slick and ready for his dick.

"Lie back."

Vincenzo liked ordering her around. She lay back against his sheets, her brown hair fanning out against his pillow, looking so innocent, beautiful, and pure.

He had no right to fuck her. To make her his. He didn't intend to keep her or have her in his life. This was going to be the one and only night they were together. But he couldn't resist.

Kneeling between her spread thighs, he kissed her lips, working his way down her body. She wriggled beneath him, arching up, moaning as he glided down, going to her pussy. She had a fine dusting of hair, but he didn't mind. He hated it when women were completely bare. Spreading the lips of her pussy open, he stared at her swollen clit.

Licking his lips, he wanted a taste.

She would be all his.

****

The first swipe of Vincenzo's tongue and Arika was in heaven. At first, she tensed up because she didn't know what was coming, and then she moaned. His tongue moved up and down, around her clit, then over it. The pleasure took her higher and higher, making her ache for more.

She felt that building heat and need coiling its way inside her, making her want to come.

"That's right, baby, come all over my face."

Whatever he was doing, she couldn't deny him. That feeling kept on building until there was nothing left, and she cried out his name, coming as he stroked her over and over. She came hard, and Vincenzo kept on licking her pussy, driving her wild with need.

"Yes, yes, yes," she said, begging for more.

He brought her down over her peak and her body tingled all over. She couldn't believe what had just happened. She felt ... sated. Like she'd been waiting a long time and finally knew what to expect.

"That felt amazing."

"Good." He moved between her thighs. He rested on one hand, and the other teased between her thighs, stroking her pussy. "You're nice and wet for me. I'm so sorry, Arika. This is going to hurt."

Before she could think or do anything, his cock was at her entrance and he slammed in deep, taking her by surprise with the force of it. She cried out, arching up as he tore through her virginity, laying claim to that part of herself she couldn't give to anyone else. His hands went to her hips, seating himself to the hilt.

She stared up at him, tears flooding her eyes.

Pain was between her thighs as he held himself still.

He'd warned her, and she knew.

"I am sorry."

He pressed a kiss to her lips.

She didn't push him away. Reaching out, she wrapped her arms around his neck, pulling him in close, kissing him hard.

Vincenzo didn't give her long to recover from

that first initial thrust. He pulled out of her and started to rock back and forth. She felt every single inch of him as he took her, going in deeper, harder.

When he started to fuck her and the bed slammed against the wall with each repeated thrust, she realized he had been going easier on her, trying to let her get accustomed to the length of his cock along with the width.

He tilted her hips, and each thrust she felt inside her like a red-hot brand. The pain lessened to be replaced by that burning heat she had just moments ago.

"You feel so fucking tight. I knew you'd be perfect. My pretty little virgin."

"I'm not anymore."

"You're all mine, Arika, and don't you forget it." He pulled back, lifting her so that her ass was on his thighs. The angle showed his cock filling her, fucking her. The red on his cock was that of her virgin blood, surprising her. He was also slick with her own arousal as well.

She was turned on by his brand of ownership as he held her down and took what he wanted.

"Watch me as I take you. Make you mine."

Arika stared down between her thighs, seeing his cock pushing in and out of her. He was so big. She was surprised he fit at all, but that was the beauty of them both. He'd fit regardless.

With her gaze on his cock, his hand moved between the lips of pussy and started to tease her. His fingers glided between them, touching near her entrance where he was sliding in and out, then up over her clit.

The pleasure was instant and intense.

She closed her eyes, unable to handle too much.

"Watch me, Arika. Watch this." He pinched her clit, and she cried out from the pleasurable pain he administered. Spreading her legs wider, she tried to get closer to him. One of his hands held her hip to the point that she knew without a doubt there'd be bruises on her skin. Not that it was a problem, far from it.

He continued to thrust in and out of her, taking her to new heights as he stroked her clit, making her take both and to watch what he did.

Nothing made any sense to her.

She couldn't think.

Just feel the heat of pleasure as it built within her, driving her higher and higher toward that peak of no return.

She couldn't stop it.

Holding onto the blanket beneath her she tried to keep her sanity, but it was no use. There was nothing else she could do, and as he stroked over her clit one final time, she came hard, screaming his name.

Vincenzo didn't slow down. He didn't back up. He kept on teasing her, prolonging her climax until it was at the point of pain. Only when she could stand it no more did he release her.

Now he took her hands, slamming her to the bed, holding them above her head, locking them within his own grip and keeping her captive.

She didn't think it was possible for him to be holding anything back, but as he looked into her eyes and then started to *really* fuck her, she knew he'd been taking it easy on her.

With her second climax she'd gotten wetter, and now he slid in deep and she cried out his name, needing him, begging for him, desperate as he took her body, fucking her hard, pounding inside her. His cock hit the hilt within her each and every single time, making her forget that only moments ago she was a virgin.

She belonged to him now.

His cock slid deep inside her, making her ache, moan, and be desperate for more.

Over and over, he slammed in hard, driving her need for him higher.

She had never known what all the fuss was about.

Being held under him, she finally understood it and knew she'd made a big fucking mistake.

Tonight was only supposed to be a one-time deal. She didn't know if she'd ever be able to have this as one time. This felt so good.

As he drove inside her that last time, she felt his cock pulse, filling her pussy with wave upon wave of heat. He groaned, pressing his lips against the side of her neck, sucking on her pulse.

Tomorrow, no matter what, she'd have marks.

Proof of what they'd done.

She didn't care.

Closing her eyes, she basked in his surrounding heat, never wanting him to stop, needing him more than anything. She clearly wasn't normal. There's no way she could be this obsessed with a man who killed people, but she was.

He pulled away from her, releasing her arms, withdrawing from her pussy, and she watched a little shocked as he left the room without a backward glance.

Vincenzo didn't say anything, and she was a little hurt.

There's no way she'd wait around for him to come back. She had to get out of there. He didn't want her here.

She didn't want to deal with the morning-after routine or what happened once the fun happy time had ended.

Even as she ached a lot, she ignored that pain and rushed back out into the hallway. Finding her bra and dress, she held up the remains of her thong and tsked, throwing it to one side.

She was just about to secure the bra when it was suddenly pulled from her grip.

"Where the fuck do you think you're going?"

"I'm leaving. We're done, right?"

"We're nowhere near done." He pulled her into his arms. "I can't give you more than tonight." His lips grazed her shoulder. "But I said the full night."

She glanced across the room seeing the lonely digital clock on the wall. It was a little past eleven o'clock. Not that late at all.

"I'll take you home tomorrow, but I've still got a lot I want to do to you and I'm going to, baby. This body needs a good fucking, and I'm the perfect guy for the job." He slid his hand between her thighs, touching her sensitive pussy. "You've got blood and cum all over you, sweetheart. I didn't think you'd like it if I flipped you over and fucked you from behind without cleaning you up first. You'll be sore tomorrow, but you won't be at work."

"I will be."

"You're off. I've already called your boss. He's got someone else to work your shift. You'll take tomorrow off to deal with whatever soreness, and until then, your body is mine to do with as I please."

With that, he picked her up and carried her back to the bathroom.

She should protest.

Arika didn't say a word as he lowered her into the tub. She didn't want to. This may only be one night, but to her it was going to be the best night of her life.

Chapter Eight

Vincenzo had never known a pussy to be so fucking tight. He watched Arika as she lay back in the tub. The hot water was clearly helping whatever aches he may have given her. Her eyes were closed, so he could look without fear of her seeing something or of hoping for something.

This was going to be one night.

It didn't matter that he was fucking happy to see her.

Or that she made his dick hard.

Or even that he was addicted to the scent and sight of her.

None of it mattered because tonight was a one-time deal and he intended to get his fill of her. To sate his hunger and then move on. To forget about her. She was just one woman in a world full of them.

She didn't hold any magical ability to keep him sated.

It didn't matter that she'd been a virgin.

No other man had touched her, tasted her, fucked her.

A complete and total innocent.

None of that could mean anything come the morning.

She'd have to go, and he'd have to move on with his life.

There were jobs to do.

"I had no idea you were at the club tonight," she said.

Her eyes opened, and she smiled.

"Why were you there?"

"Rachel was under the impression that I needed to get laid, which is why we were there. I guess she was right."

"That bar is not the best place to pick up men, Arika."

"I picked you up."

"I'm one of a kind."

"And what makes you one of a kind?" she asked.

"Simple. I've no intention of hurting you. You know the kind of people I run with. They visit that club often, and I don't want you part of this life."

"Which is why it's a one-night deal."

"Exactly. You can't go getting romantic notions about what is happening between us."

She burst out laughing. "I'm not going to get romantic notions or think that you love me, Vincenzo. I'm not ... I'm under no illusions, okay? Have you ever thought that I may like this? That just having sex works for me?"

"Does it?"

"Yes. I've got a plan, remember? I don't need a man to live that. I'm working hard on finishing college right now."

"You'll do well in life, I'm sure of it." He stood up and moved toward the bath. He reached in and pulled the plug.

"Hey, what are you doing?"

"You've had enough fun. One night only, remember. I want your pussy again and so much more."

He grabbed a towel, wrapping it around her and picking her up.

"You're crazy, you know that?"

"I've killed men for less than that insult. However, coming from you, I find it rather cute."

She burst out laughing, and damn he loved that sound.

Carrying her through to his bedroom, he put her

on the floor, drying off her body and hair.

Once he was done, he threw the towel out of his way, cupped her face, and kissed her hard.

She opened up to him, her hand flat against his stomach.

He took hold of her wrist, moving her down to cup his already hard, aching cock. When he'd gone into the bathroom he'd washed himself.

Breaking the kiss, he stared into her pretty brown eyes.

"Let's put that mouth to some good use." He pressed on her shoulders, and she sank to her knees before him. "Now that is a very pretty sight."

Running his fingers through her hair, he wrapped the length around his wrist, pulling her back and her mouth slid open. Placing a thumb onto her lips, he pushed in and out. "Suck it, Arika. Show me what you'll do to my cock."

Her lips closed around his thumb, and she sucked him in, taking him as deep as his hand would let her.

"Don't use teeth," he said.

She stopped scoring her teeth down his thumb, and after a few practice sucks, he smiled. She had the hang of what he wanted.

Removing his thumb, he placed the tip of his cock to her lips. "Open."

She opened her lips, and he slid in, spreading her pink lips wide, and he was right. They did look so good spread around his cock.

"Get it nice and wet. Lick it."

She covered his cock in her saliva, getting him exactly how he wanted, wet, and as he thrust back into her mouth, he hit her throat.

He did this a couple of times, letting her get accustomed to the feel of him going that far.

After a few minutes of this, he hit the back of her throat and didn't pull back. Staring into her eyes, he waited and her eyes went wide, but she didn't fight him.

With his grip in her hair, he held her in place, and then pressed another inch inside her mouth.

"Relax. Don't panic. I'm not going to hurt you."

She gagged, and he pulled back. Still holding her hair, he pushed again, and this time, he got a little further before she gagged. Her hands went to his thighs, her nails biting into his flesh, but that was okay.

Over and over, he got her used to him hitting her throat, making her take him, watching those lips stretch around his dick like they were supposed to. She looked so fucking beautiful, so perfect, and he couldn't resist her.

Fucking her mouth, he changed it up from making her deep throat him to shallow thrusts. His cock was completely coated in her saliva.

He felt the first stirrings of his orgasm start to build.

"I'm going to come in your mouth, and when I do, I don't want you to swallow."

Her eyes once again went wide, but she did as he asked.

As he came, he held the tip in her mouth, her lips covering his length holding him inside her as wave upon wave of cum filled her mouth. He waited until every single last drop was done with before pulling out from between her lips.

She pressed them together.

"Show me."

She frowned at him.

"Tilt your head back and show me."

She tilted her head back and then slowly opened her mouth. There, pooling, was his cum.

Wrapping his fingers around her lips, he watched. "Swallow it."

She did so, and he watched it disappear.

Fucking beautiful.

****

Arika couldn't believe she had just done that and not only done it, but also enjoyed it. She loved how he ordered her around. The darkness swirling in his gaze. The temptation he gave her by just giving her orders.

Vincenzo lifted her up from the floor, his lips grazing across her collarbone before he moved her to the bed.

He pushed her down, going with her. His cock, now flaccid, was pressing against her body. He wasn't hard yet, but she didn't imagine he would be for a little time. She'd taken every single drop like he'd demanded, and it had surprised her how much he had come.

He nipped at her neck, his lips trailing down to suck on one tit then the other before moving back to the first one.

She took his weight as he pushed her tits together, licking, sucking, and biting at her nipples. Each tug and bite seemed to make her clit ache for more. Her body was so sensitive and so alive for more of his touch. She couldn't get enough.

He didn't just suck at her nipples though.

She watched as he licked and nipped the sides of her breasts before moving down to her pussy. His tongue slid across her clit, and she thrust up, wanting more. He held her legs open, and he concentrated on her clit, not going anywhere else, just her clit, doing the same to her nub as he'd done to every other part of her body.

Arika didn't know how much time had passed. She was getting so wet that she felt it spilling from her pussy, moving down the crack of her ass.

Vincenzo suddenly pulled away as he flipped her over, moving her to her knees.

Pressing her face against the pillow she gasped as his finger slid inside her. He followed with a second, pushing in and out, stretching her pussy.

He didn't linger for long, and she tensed up as he brought those slick fingers out and started to tease her anus.

"I'm going to fuck this, Arika. When you leave me tonight I will take every single hole and make it mine. Not a part of you will be untouched."

She was nervous but knew she wanted this.

Whatever he wanted to do to her, she was more than ready, desperate even, for his touch.

He began to circle her anus, pressing against the puckered hole.

She gritted her teeth, not wanting him to slide inside her and yet wanting him to as well. It felt dirty, wrong, and yet it was also utterly right.

"Relax, baby."

His other hand cupped her pussy so he was working her pussy and ass at the same time. One finger slid inside her as the other pressed against the tight ring of muscles, begging to be let in.

She couldn't fight against the pleasure and gave herself up to it, relaxing. He pushed inside her to the knuckle, going in deep.

She cried out at the initial intrusion, somewhat shocked by the feel of him in her pussy and ass.

The finger in her pussy moved out, stroking over her clit as the one in her ass moved in and out.

"That's it, Arika. Feel me."

The sensations were different, but they were also taken over by the pleasure as he continued to tease her clit.

When he added a second finger to her ass, she gasped.

He took his time, working her, stretching her. He made her moan as the pain morphed into pleasure, making her want so much more.

When he added in a third finger, opening her up, she couldn't believe she was taking it.

"You're so wet for me, baby. You're going to take my cock so easily."

She moaned again, and as he stroked her pussy, she couldn't find a single argument to disagree with him. She wanted his cock. She wanted this.

He stroked her clit, moving down to plunge inside her as his other hand stretched her anus, getting her used to being touched there.

Tomorrow would be a hard day for her, but it was going to be so worth it. There was no way she could stop this.

She'd imagined this for so long.

Had wanted it for even longer.

She couldn't say no.

Not now.

"So fucking pretty. I wish you could see this. Your asshole opening up. Don't worry, it'll go tight back together, but right now it wants a nice big cock inside it. Fuck, that is pretty."

She turned her head, and with all the mirrors, she saw him staring at her ass, his finger stretching her.

The pleasure to her third orgasm was building, and she closed her eyes once again, feeling his touch, basking in what he was doing to her body again.

She'd dreamed of feeling something like this.

Of having a man do what he wanted with her, and she was a mere puppet in his hands. He teased her body, drove her crazy with need, and as she came for the third time that night, she screamed his name, not wanting to let him go even though she knew she'd have to.

Everything he was doing to her, she wanted more than anything.

She'd pushed all of her fantasies to one side and all that left was the two of them.

****

Arika's pussy was dripping wet.

Her asshole was nice and ready for him.

Vincenzo couldn't get e-fucking-nough of this woman. Her body was a dream to him. A blank canvas he could work with, make his own.

This was supposed to be a one-time deal, just tonight where he got to fuck her every which way he wanted. Tomorrow, she'd go back to her life, and he'd go back to his.

He hoped after he'd taken every single virginity she possessed that he still wasn't thinking about her or craving her.

This life with him wasn't for the fainthearted. It was a hard life. A cruel life, but a life he'd been living and one he couldn't just walk away from.

Gripping his cock, he placed it at the entrance of her pussy and slid in deep. Their combined releases coated his dick, slicking him up, ready to take her.

He fucked her three times and pulled out, placing the tip where his fingers had been moments before.

Her asshole wasn't used to this kind of intrusion, and tomorrow she'd hurt but she'd remember this.

Slowly, inch by inch, he sank inside her ass.

She cried out, and he paused, letting her get used to this.

Her ass was nothing like her pussy.

He didn't want to hurt her, and if he wasn't careful and she fought him, he could do some serious damage to her anus. The point of tonight was not only to sate his own needs but to also drive her crazy as well.

Sliding in and out, he fucked her, driving her higher with every single push, not going to deep, only letting her grow wild with a few inches.

When she could take what he could give her and she started to thrust back, he pushed more of his dick within her, watching it disappear inside her ass. She was tight as well, incredibly so.

This woman was made for his cock. Made for him in every single way.

Pushing his cock to the hilt within her tight ass, he held himself there. Wrapping his arms around her body, he lifted her up so that her back was pressed against his front. Kissing her shoulder, he glanced in the mirror in front of them.

Her eyes were squeezed tight.

"Look at me," he said.

She opened her eyes, and gasped.

"You look so fucking hot. My dick is deep inside your ass right now. Where it should be." In response her ass tightened around his length, and he hissed out. "So tight. You want me to fuck you."

She nodded.

"Let me hear you say it."

"Yes."

"Yes, what?"

"Yes, I want you to fuck my ass."

"Baby, you are so perfect. You don't even realize at times just how amazing you are."

He let her go, wrapping his hand in her hair as he started to pull out of her ass, and staring at his slick cock, he thrust back in. They both cried out.

Vincenzo took his time, letting her get used to the feel of him inside her, fucking her, taking her, driving her wild.

She was made for fucking.

Her body was so perfect for his cock, the way her pussy had opened up for him, her mouth swallowing his cum, and now her ass taking his dick.

She'd be the perfect woman to come home to, to look forward to seeing at the end of a long, hard day.

One night.

Only one night.

He couldn't have more than this moment.

Taking her ass, he waited for that special moment as she pushed back against him, going just a little deeper.

She drove backward, fucking him back, and he knew he had her.

Her face had gone from one of pain and pleasure to just one of absolute rapture. Releasing her hair, he gripped her hips and slapped her ass, taking her, pounding inside her anus so she knew who she belonged to.

No one else was ever going to compare to him.

She could live her happy life, but she'd always know he was out there, what he could to do her body, and in this moment, he was going to be a selfish fucking bastard because he didn't want to share her with anyone.

If he couldn't have her completely, then he was going to take what little piece he could. All of her first times so any man that came after, she'd always think of him. It was the most selfish thing he'd ever done, and he didn't even feel remorse for it.

She belonged to him, and nothing was ever going to keep them apart.

Not now, not ever.

He took what he wanted, and when he came, he slid to the hilt and spilled wave upon wave of his cum deep in her ass, making her take it.

This time once he came, he didn't pull away.

He covered her body, wrapping his arms around her, holding her against him as his cock slowly grew flaccid.

"Are you hurt?" he asked.

"Sore, but I can handle that."

"We need to wash," he said. Slowly withdrawing from her, he climbed off the bed but not before seeing his cum spilling from between her ass cheeks. Now that was a pretty sight. He didn't linger, heading back into his bathroom, running a fresh bath with extra salts. He walked back to the bedroom and picked her up in his arms.

She held onto him, and he didn't leave her this time or sit out of the bath.

He joined her, pulling her against his chest, knowing this was the last moment he'd feel this.

He didn't like that bolt of pain that struck him knowing someone else would be with her soon. There would be a man who'd know what a precious gem she was, and Vincenzo was just going to have to live with that.

Kissing the top of her head, he held her close.

These were the moments he'd cherish for himself. She knew a lot about him, and she didn't push him away. Nothing else mattered. Just this.

Chapter Nine

"We found this sniveling little shit lurking behind one of the crates at our shipment. He had this in his hands." One of Galiza's sons held up a camera, about to destroy it.

"Don't do that," Vincenzo said.

"You're telling me what to do?"

"I'm telling you not to destroy his camera."

"It's got fucking evidence on it of our shipment of coke."

"Or it could have evidence as to who else has been leaking information to the cops," Vincenzo said.

That's what the Galizas were having to deal with right now. Their businesses throughout the city were being raided. Men and women were being arrested, and some of them were ending up in the river.

Most people were pointing at the Vitale family.

Vincenzo didn't for a second believe it was another family getting the law involved. This was an inside job, and he had a feeling someone was trying for a takeover of Galiza's place. If there was enough proof that Galiza wasn't strong enough to hold the family together, then there would be a vote of no confidence and he would be removed from his spot.

Staring at one of Galiza's sons, Vincenzo had a feeling it could be one of them.

"We don't need whatever this fucking rat has to offer," Galiza said.

"Then why bring us in?" Daniel asked, speaking up from his little corner. They had been called to come to the warehouse down at the docks. It was over a three-hour drive from the city, and Vincenzo hadn't wanted to come here to deal with this shit, especially as he didn't trust any of Galiza's sons. They all had a potential motive for going after their father.

It's why he didn't trust them.

Any one of them could want their father's place and in doing so, feed enough evidence to the cops to put pressure on their father. Of course, he didn't have any proof.

"Who do you think you're talking to, soldier?" The oldest Galiza glared at Daniel.

"Clearly, you want this fucker dead without talking."

"We want him to talk."

"Then hand over the camera. That's part of him talking as well," Daniel said.

"If we don't have that camera, I'm not helping with this," Vincenzo said.

"You're a fucking minion, Barbato. You will do as you're told."

"I'm your father's fucking minion, not yours. I don't take orders from a baby."

"That is quite enough," the head Galiza said, entering the warehouse.

Vincenzo watched Galiza's sons, waiting or trying to find a sign that they were guilty or shocked to see him. When he'd gotten the call to come to the docks, he'd called the head Galiza himself to find out the truth.

Galiza had been shocked to discover he was wanted at the docks and had agreed to be there at some point.

"Dad, what are you doing here?"

"You don't think I know what goes down at my own dock? When my weapon is called to do business, I know what is going on. That is the camera he was using?"

"Yes, Dad, but we don't—"

"Give it to fucking Daniel now. I'm tired of this

bullshit. You want Vincenzo to do his job but take part of what he needs. Give him the fucking camera."

The camera was thrown in Daniel's direction.

Vincenzo watched as his guard caught it and smiled. It had been thrown in such a way that it could have been smashed.

"I used to play ball back in the day," Daniel said.

Yeah, he was getting more and more convinced that one of these fuckers was behind the constant raids and law problems they were having.

He'd even gotten pulled over just the other day and had to give his license and registration. The cop had been shitting himself, but Vincenzo had known something was up then.

"Good, now, let's see how a master handles something like this. You may take over, Vincenzo."

The man in the chair whimpered. "Please, I don't know anything."

Moving away from his space, Vincenzo walked in front of the man.

"Do you know who I am?"

"You're the mafia's dog. Their weapon. You hurt everyone and everything."

For a split second he thought about Arika. He didn't know why she flashed in his mind. The morning after the night they shared together, as promised, he'd dropped her off at her apartment.

No kisses.

No goodbyes.

One night of smoking hot sex and that had been the end of it.

Pushing her to the back of his mind, he looked at the man sitting in front of him. Grabbing a chair, he heard someone sigh.

"He's going to have some fun," Daniel said.

Straddling the chair, Vincenzo looked at the guy. He didn't even recognize him.

"You got any family?" Vincenzo asked.

"No. None."

"Are you lying to me?"

"I'm a reporter. I don't have family. It's too dangerous." He sobbed out the last part, clearly knowing he wasn't going to leave this dock alive.

"So, are you going to tell me everything I need to know?"

"I don't know anything. I promise."

"But you came to this dock." He reached into his jacket and looked at his wallet. "And you're about six hours out of your way from where you live." He threw his ID at him, then his credit cards. "Your life is nowhere near this dock, so you had to travel here."

"We don't need to—"

"Why don't you shut the fuck up?" Galiza said. "Let him do his job."

"I wanted pecan pancakes this morning with chocolate chips and syrup. There's a restaurant that serves really good pancakes. You ask the right person, they make them when you arrive and serve them hot with warm maple syrup. Delicious. I was going to go there this morning."

"Shit, you haven't had your pancakes?" Daniel asked.

"I've not had a single bite to eat."

"Damn, this is not going to go easy for you. Not in the slightest. You should have at least let the guy have his coffee."

"I don't know anything. I was told to be at a time and at a place. I promise."

Vincenzo hated it when grown men became bumbling pussies. Getting up from his chair, he made his way toward the briefcase he'd brought with him. There was a table in the corner, and he placed it near the man bound to the chair. Picking up his briefcase, he placed it on the flat surface, doing the code that would unlock it.

"I'm very old school, I am," he said, removing his tools from the briefcase and putting them on the table. Opening out the case, it showed some of his tools from a variety of knives to pliers and other pieces of equipment perfect as a personal torture kit. "You know I went to college. Took several classes in human biology and of course medicine as well. What makes these two arts fascinating is I learned exactly what body part I can take and also how to keep a person alive long enough to make them talk but to also tell me all of their secrets." He grabbed the man's hand and, with the clippers, snipped off the man's ring finger.

The screams echoed around the warehouse.

Vincenzo was used to them.

They ran off him like water in a shower. This was what he'd been trained to do, knew nothing else and wouldn't ever change who he was.

"Fuck! Please, please, no more."

"Wow, he's already pissed himself," Daniel said.

"How long have you been in contact with this person?" He believed this man didn't have a clue who'd called him. The truth of the person's identity would come in the finer details. It was amazing how a person sounded, what they said, what their instructions were. He knew when he got the call today that Galiza had nothing to do with this. That he didn't even have a fucking clue about it.

The finer details.

It was what torture was all about.

Learning those little facts.

The reporter gave up very little, and what little he

did have, wouldn't lead them to find out any more clues. Someone close to Galiza was doing this, but it was a smokescreen to hide something. Vincenzo had an idea who was behind the reporter's sudden appearance, but he wasn't willing to call out a traitor without actual proof.

He slit the guy's throat, waiting for him to die and then removed his eyes.

"Why the fuck did you do that?" the oldest Galiza asked.

"Simple. His body will be discovered, and every single reporter will know if they work to bring down the Galiza in any way they will answer for their crimes. Be careful what you look for, I'll be coming."

"You did wonderful," Galiza said, coming to him, slapping him on the back.

"I need to look at his camera, and I'll need forty-eight hours to go and check out his apartment."

"Do what you need to do. I'll keep his body on ice until then."

With that, he left the warehouse with Daniel in tow.

"What are you thinking?" Daniel asked.

"It's one of them in there," Vincenzo said.

"The sons?"

"Yep."

"Why?"

"Power. To overthrow their father. I don't really care who it is. I just know we've got to find the one responsible."

"Why now?"

"Because we've got that camera and the resources. I'd start watching your back, Daniel. They'll come after us next."

****

Arika's feet hurt, but that was to be expected after

a ten-hour shift with no break in between. They'd been swamped with customers, and that was a good thing. No customers, no work. Lots of customers, plenty of work.

She liked working.

It helped to take her mind off everything else going on in her life.

School.

Studies.

Life.

Him.

She tried not to think about him.

He'd not been wrong about his plan. It truly had been a one-night affair.

It had certainly been a night she wouldn't be forgetting any time soon. She'd been fucked in every single way that mattered, and now he'd ruined her for anyone else. Rachel was constantly trying to set her up with someone, and Arika turned her down flat. The last thing she wanted right now was to date anyone.

Walking up the stairs to her apartment, she stood outside and worked the three different locks. Stepping inside, she quickly locked the three and bolted the rest from the inside. If anyone tried to break down her door, they could just splinter the wood with enough force. At least it gave her some semblance of being protected. Not a lot but enough.

Flicking on the light, she turned around and froze.

"I could have been anyone," he said.

"Anyone wouldn't have snuck into someone's apartment," she said. "How did you get in here?"

"I have a key."

She saw Vincenzo held a set of keys within his grasp. "This isn't even a little bit funny."

"I'm not laughing. I find your safety important."

"I thought that was the reason I wouldn't see you

again. My safety."

"It seems that I may have hit a bit of a snag."

"Snag?"

"Yes. You see. One night wasn't enough for me. Take off your jacket."

"No."

He raised his brow.

"You're not supposed to be here."

"You want me to leave?"

"I want to know why you're here?"

"I'm here because I want to fuck you again, Arika. Tell me in the past two weeks you've not thought about me?"

She licked her lips, refusing to confirm or deny him.

"You have thought about me. Don't worry, sweetheart. You don't need to say anything. I can see the truth in your eyes. I was the first man in that tight little cunt, ass, and mouth. I'll answer first. I've done nothing but think about you."

"How many women have you been with while you've been thinking about me?" she asked.

She wouldn't be jealous. There's no way she'd give him that kind of power again.

"None."

"None?"

"That's right. Have you had any men trying to come and take what is mine?"

"No."

He gave her that smirk, which she hated.

"I've been busy."

"You can blame your lack of fucking of other men on anything you want, but you and I both know it's because you want me. No man will ever match up to your first."

"So, I won't match up to the other women you've been with?" she asked.

"It's a little different for men. Women have a tendency to blend in together."

"Charming."

"Unless of course there's *one* woman. Take off your clothes, Arika. I know you want my mouth on that pretty pussy. I can see it in your eyes."

He stood up, but he didn't make a move toward her.

She watched as he removed his jacket, then began to unbutton his shirt.

"You're so sure about this."

"When it comes to you, I can read you like a book. You want my cock. You just don't like that you want to use me as much as I want to use you, and believe me, I do. I want to fuck you until you can't think straight."

The shirt fell to the floor, and he kicked off his shoes then his trousers until he stood naked.

He then sat down on her rather threadbare sofa. She did have a throw over it to hide how worn the fabric was. He wrapped his fingers around his dick, running his hand up and down the length. The tip glistened with pre-cum.

She remembered what it felt like to have him in her mouth. To suck on his dick, to feel him filling her with his cum before swallowing it all.

"There's nothing wrong with using each other. You've not found a man. No one knows I'm here so you're more than safe. Come on, Arika. Use me. Make me fuck you. Let me show you how much I've missed you. There's nothing wrong with taking your pleasure how you want it."

Pulling her bag off over her head, she then

removed her jacket.

She hated how accurate he was. How much she had missed him. The fact that every single night she'd brought herself to orgasm with just the memory of him, pissed her off. She didn't want him to have any kind of power over her, and yet, it seemed that no matter what she did, he owned a part of her.

He was her first.

The best moments of her life.

Driving her completely wild.

She'd wake up in the middle of the night, aching, sweat-slicked, desperate.

Opening the dress of her uniform, she stepped out of it, kicking off her shoes. Stepping closer to him, she removed her underwear.

Standing just out of his reach, she glared at him.

"This doesn't mean that every single time you want to get your rocks off, you can come here."

"Baby, I don't just want to get my rocks off. I want to get my dick off." He reached out, grabbing her hand and tugging her close.

She stepped toward him, staring into his eyes as his hand went between her thighs. She opened her legs and moaned as he started to finger-fuck her pussy, stroking inside her, pulling out to tease her clit. He circled her bud, flicking his finger back and forth, making her even more wet.

He pushed two fingers inside her, and she started to work herself onto them.

"That's right. See, you want this as well. I can give you what you want, Arika, and I take what I want."

When she was close to coming, he pulled out.

She growled his name, but he didn't make her wait long. He pulled her over his thighs so that she was straddling him. Vincenzo took the lead. Putting his cock at her entrance, he slowly began to fill her. She thrust down, taking him in. It was a tight fit but nothing like the pain she experienced that first time.

Gripping onto his shoulders, she lifted herself up then moved back down, making him go deep.

They both moaned.

Vincenzo's hands went from her hips to her ass, then up to cup her tits.

"I can't get enough of you. I want you constantly. I stroke my cock thinking about you in the morning. I wake up so hard remembering how fucking hot you looked with a mouthful of cum. You loved it, didn't you, Arika? You loved me fucking you, taking what was mine."

"Yes, please, shut up. Fuck me, Vincenzo."

She cried out as he lifted her up, withdrawing his cock. He pressed her over the back of the chair. He found her entrance and slid home. His hands cupped her tits, pinching her nipples before moving down to tease her pussy.

He stroked her clit at the same time as he fucked her hard.

The sound of their bodies slapping together as well as their moans echoed around the room.

His body was everywhere. She felt completely surrounded by him, and she loved every second, desperate for more.

The moment he brought her to orgasm, Vincenzo didn't let up. He grabbed her hips and started to pound away inside her. He slapped her ass, and she pushed back against him, needing him.

"Please, yes, yes, it feels so good."

"Fuck, baby, you're so fucking sexy. So perfect. So everything."

He thrust inside her one final time, and she felt

every single spurt as his cum filled her, felt each pulse of his cock as he came, holding her tighter than ever before.

She couldn't believe they had just fucked.

Panting for breath, she closed her eyes. His lips brushed against her neck. "Thank you, Arika. That was everything I wanted."

She didn't open her eyes as he pulled away nor as he finished getting dressed. She stayed in position with his cum dripping down her thighs. She didn't move until she heard the door close.

Arika pushed her hair off her face and relocked her door again.

She knew she should deny him, but she would also be denying herself. As much as it hurt to hear him walk away, she didn't want it to stop.

Chapter Ten

Daniel bit into his large cheeseburger with all the trimmings. "That was a big fucking bust. The camera and his place both. None of it makes sense. Did that guy really get killed for a big fucking hunch?"

Vincenzo looked through the pictures again.

There was nothing on the dead reporter's camera that could have been worth anything. There were pictures of Galiza and of his sons. Looking at them from different angles, he rubbed at his eyes.

"You've got that look as if to say you're pissed."

"Don't talk with your mouth full."

"Wow, sorry, Dad. I didn't realize I was offending you. You do know that for the past two weeks we've been running around chasing a dead end, right?" Daniel asked. "The cops have stopped the raids, and even the Vitale have gone silent as well. It's like this whole shitstorm was a mask."

"Yeah, for something bigger." Vincenzo took a bite of his hot dog and looked back over the pictures. The sun was shining, and other than spending a lot of time with Daniel, his day was going rather well.

Galiza had him working the Vitale link as well as the raids, but he'd also been asked by his boss to keep it quiet. That if he was asked what he was working on, just to say stuff. It was rare for him to get such private work like now. Most of the time the entire family knew the drill, which told him Galiza believed it was close.

He really needed to figure out the connection. He didn't know if his boss would even think about executing one of his sons if it was ever discovered they had tried to kill him.

Vincenzo hadn't been around for any inner family conflict like that.

"You've got that thinking head on," Daniel said. "Out with it."

"What if our rat is working with the Vitale?" Vincenzo said.

"Nah, that's not possible."

"Why not?"

"The Vitale are fucking assholes, man. Years ago, I'm talking when we were little boys in diapers, the Vitale had an equal share in controlling the city. It was a bloodbath. I remember my dad saying that men would see women in the street, and it didn't matter who they were with, if they wanted them, they'd take them. Kids were dying. Families were being killed for even looking at them. It was a fucking war. A bloodbath. The Vitale were too power-hungry."

"Yeah, and to have support when their head family ends up dead. To reunite two families. Doesn't Vitale have a daughter?"

"Yeah, so?"

"Bring two families together in marriage. You can no longer bring about a war or crush a family in that instance. I want a meeting set up with their torturer."

"You think that's wise?"

"I know Gabe. He's a tough fucker but a fair man. We've met a few times. Set it up."

"Like that. Treating me as your damn secretary."

"What else would I treat you as?" he asked.

"I don't know. Friend, colleague maybe."

"Daniel, you have all the numbers. I don't need to stroke your fucking ego right now. It's the last thing I want to do, got it?"

Daniel rolled his eyes. "So, you seen anything of that chick yet?"

"Chick?"

"You know. Wrong girl, wrong time. She got on

the other end of my gun." He held his thumb and finger up, pretending to have a gun.

"Don't fucking bring her up."

"I'll take that as a no."

"She's not part of this world."

"Is that your hang-up over that shit? This world ain't so bad."

"Were you there when the ex-mistress got tortured? Raped? You know her screams."

"Please, I've heard you draw screams out of men that curdle the blood. Besides, that whore acted out of jealousy and got what she deserved. What does that have to do with your plain chick?"

"Don't bring her up. You keep doing so, I'll cut your dick off."

"Fair, but you've got to answer my question, and if it's a good reason, I'll back off."

"So long as you figure it's a good reason."

"Pretty much."

"This life is dangerous. You see what's happening. I'm the kind of guy people go after to kill. To hunt. I'm not going to let someone hurt her because of me."

"You like her," Daniel said.

Vincenzo rolled his eyes. "I don't need to hear this bullshit."

"Doesn't take away from the fact that you clearly have feelings for this woman, otherwise you wouldn't care."

"When did we become girls talking about this?"

"You know it's fine to fall in love," Daniel said.

He looked over at his guard to see Daniel had in fact become serious. "It's not going to happen."

"She's good for you. The few weeks you were taking care of her, you were a lot happier," Daniel said.

"Damn, that is a good burger." He threw the wrappings in the trashcan next to them.

Climbing behind the wheel, Vincenzo waited for Daniel to get in before taking off.

While he drove, Daniel looked through the pictures again.

"I totally wish I know what the fuck was going on here," Daniel said. He kept turning the picture around.

"Will you fucking stop that? It's distracting."

"Hold up. Pull the fuck over," Daniel said.

"What?"

"You heard me, pull over."

Pulling against the side of the road, he glared at him. "We've got shit to do."

"Look at those two pictures," Daniel said. "Come on, man. I know I take the piss every now and again but come on. I know when I see something, and I see something now."

Taking the pictures from Daniel, Vincenzo started to look at them. "What?"

"You remember about five weeks ago, Galiza had a secret meeting? Remember? I'm telling you. That church right there is exactly where that meeting was at."

"You're positive."

"So fucking positive right now. I can guarantee that's where it was at. I swear to you, Vince. This is the place."

"If that's the case, whoever knew about this meeting was the person that told the reporter."

"Yep, so now we need to know everyone that was involved."

"I'll talk to Galiza."

"I know you and I believe this is an inside job, but will he accept that it is?"

"He's got no choice."

"Vince, you're looking at one of his sons. I know he's an asshole most of the time, but it's still one of his sons. His flesh and blood."

"Look, this is going to be a decision he has to make. We can only point him in the right direction." Vincenzo ran fingers through his hair. "I'll talk to him."

"You still want me to set up the meeting with Gabe?"

"Yeah."

Whichever way this went, there was a huge chance this was going to get really, really ugly.

Pulling away from the curb, he headed back toward the city.

He thought about Arika and what she was doing. He did keep a tab on her even at a distance. In order for him to keep her safe, they couldn't be together. No matter how much he craved her. Going to her apartment had been a big fucking mistake, something he shouldn't have done. It had been a long day. At the time he didn't want to go back home to where the memory of her still lingered. He'd wanted to be selfish and to have her to himself.

Women had come and gone from his life. He used them for a bit of pleasure and walked away.

The last time he was with Arika, he knew he had to walk away, as otherwise he wouldn't leave her. He didn't understand these feelings, and keeping her at a distance was the only option. For the first time in his life, he felt for another human being. All of his life, he'd not cared about anyone or anything. He'd done more to end lives.

Arika was the first person he'd ever saved.

He didn't know what would have happened that night if it had been anyone else. If he'd have shot them and left them for dead. It didn't matter now. Arika had been the one shot, no one else.

He dropped Daniel off where he needed to be and made his way back across town. Pulling up outside of a jewelry store, he climbed out, and went to see if anything caught his eye. Women loved diamonds and jewelry.

Entering the shop, he saw a piece that instantly reminded him of Arika. It was a simple heart-shaped necklace that was sweet without drawing the eye. He bought it without batting an eye at the price. Next, he went to a florist and made sure they delivered the necklace and some roses.

After he'd fucked her body and left, it was the least he could do.

****

Arika smiled across the table at her *date*. She thought the word lightly. Jesse was one of Rachel's friends who she'd been asking constantly for her to go out with. On a Friday night rather than work overtime she sat opposite this rather nice-looking man. He seemed kind of nervous considering he was Rachel's friend.

"So, Arika, what do you hope to do when you … erm…"

"Grow up?" Arika asked.

"That's not what I meant. Not in the slightest. Rachel told me you were going to college, and you know, putting two and two together I put my foot in it."

She chuckled. "Well, I'm not completely decided. I've thought about teaching and then about writing. I don't know. I'm taking an English degree at the local college. I don't do it full-time as I have to work, but I love studying."

"And you love English. Please just stop me."

"It's fine. This is really nice," she said. "This restaurant."

"Thank you. It's Italian, and who doesn't love

it?"

She forced a smile, instantly thinking about Vincenzo.

Very bad move.

Very, very bad.

She wasn't a big fan of pasta or this restaurant. Sipping her wine, she smiled at him. "So, what do you do, Jesse?"

"Rachel didn't tell you?"

She shook her head. "I got, 'He's a great guy. You're going to love him. Everyone loves him.'"

Jesse's face went bright red. "I wouldn't say everyone loves me. I'm an accountant. Don't worry though. I won't bore you with all the details."

"That must be ... challenging?" She laughed. "I really don't know what else to say to that."

"It's numbers. A lot of numbers. The pleasure of your company is certainly a refreshing change."

"Thank you."

He held up his wineglass, and she clinked her glass with his.

Out of the corner of her eye, she spotted something and wasn't entirely sure what. Glancing over Jesse's shoulder, she froze. Vincenzo was sitting at a table with a blonde in front of him.

Biting her lip, she forced herself to look away.

"What's wrong?" Jesse asked.

"Nothing. Nothing at all, why?"

"Do you know someone?"

"No. This is the first time I've been to this restaurant. There's no one here I could possibly know. So, accounting? You must meet all kinds of interesting people."

Jesse started talking, and Arika tried to listen to what he said.

Inside her heart was breaking.

Was that his girlfriend?

His date?

What?

He couldn't have her in his life, but he could go on dating everyone and everything.

Don't judge.

You're on a date as well.

She had no intention of this date ending anywhere other than with a thank you. There's no way she could be jealous of Vincenzo being with someone else while she was doing the exact same thing.

Eating the pasta without really tasting it, she found herself glancing past Jesse's shoulder.

Vincenzo had seen her as well. Each time she looked in his direction, he was staring right at her.

After she finished her meal she excused herself to go to the ladies' room. Passing the tables, she steered clear of Vincenzo's, entering the bathroom. Going straight to the sink, she stared at the perfect white porcelain, her stomach twisting and turning.

"I had no idea you'd be here," Vincenzo said.

"This is the ladies' room. It's for women only." She held onto the counter. The last time she saw him, she'd vowed that no matter what, she wouldn't cave to him again.

"You looked a little upset when you left your date."

She took a deep breath and looked up at him. "What do you want from me?" she asked, staring at him through the mirror.

"I wanted to make sure you're okay."

She shook her head. "I don't know what I am, but I'm not okay. Nothing right now about any of this is okay. It's really not. You're dating someone, and I'm here with someone else." She bowed her head and felt that pain that hit her.

"This doesn't mean anything. She's work. That's all, just work."

Arika looked up at him and felt the tears in her eyes. "Then why does this hurt? It was supposed to be one night together. You can't tell me we can't be together and then be at my apartment waiting for me. Fucking me when it suits you and leaving. I don't want to be used." He went to speak, and she held her hand up. "I didn't say I didn't enjoy it. I liked it but not this. Not what happened after. It's one night or it's not, Vincenzo. What is it?" she asked.

"You're not wearing the necklace I sent."

"I'm not wearing jewelry I don't have a right to. I won't do this. Please, leave me alone."

"I've tried to leave you alone."

She closed her eyes, feeling him step closer.

When his hand landed on her hip, she didn't fight him off.

She didn't want to.

"It was supposed to be one night. One night neither of us would ever forget."

"Then back away," she said.

"I can't. I want to touch you. I think about how good you feel against me. The tightness of your pussy wrapped around my dick." His hand left her hip, moving between her thighs. She gasped as he slid beneath her panties, moving them out of the way to touch her. "Do you ache for him or for me?"

"I don't know him."

"You don't know me."

"I know enough."

"You should run the hell away from me."

"Then why can't I?" she asked. "I don't want you

to stop." He slid two fingers to the knuckles inside her, and she cried out, hungry for more of his touch. She heard the metal of his belt as he released his pants. He lifted up her skirt, tore her panties aside, and then slid in deep.

She cried out his name, knowing she should say no but hungry for more.

"Oh, fuck, baby. I knew you'd feel so good. When I saw you enter with him, I wanted to fucking kill him. You know what I'm capable of."

"You don't want me. I can't wait around forever for a one-night thing."

"This is not a one-night thing. You know that. I don't want you to go home with him."

"I'm not going to."

"Not with my cum inside you. I'm going to fuck you and then you're going to go out there, finish your dessert, go home and wait for me."

"And if I don't?"

"I will find you, Arika, and then you will wish you hadn't tested me." He fucked her hard, slamming inside her, and she pushed back, crying out and not caring if someone was to come in and see them.

She needed this.

Needed him.

He'd become her addiction, and she couldn't have enough.

He drove her crazy.

When his teeth grazed her neck and she felt his cock pulse within her, she knew coming on this date had been a huge mistake.

Staring in the mirror at their reflections, Vincenzo looked right at her.

"I want you to remember me inside you. Feel me." He pulled out of her and put her panties back into place. He rubbed his hand against her pussy, feeling his cum fall from her as he smeared it into her. "Don't disobey me."

With that, he kissed her neck, and was gone.

Returning her attention back to the sink, she fluffed up her hair, covering the spot he'd been kissing, and washed her hands, patting her cheeks with some of the cold water.

She hated going back out to her date.

Jesse was waiting.

He'd gotten her a chocolate mousse.

"Sorry I took so long."

"No problem. I was wondering how you'd feel about a walk before I take you home?"

She looked toward Vincenzo and saw him watching her.

"Erm, I'm kind of tired, to be honest. I'm so sorry. I've been up late studying."

"That's perfectly fine. I have work to do as well."

She forced a smile to her lips, hoping the meal would end.

Part of her wanted to take that walk just to piss off Vincenzo, but that didn't feel right for her to do. She had no doubt he'd hurt Jesse in some way, and she wasn't so mean-spirited to put him in that kind of danger.

When the time came for the check, she wouldn't let Jesse pay for her part. She shared the payment and followed him outside.

He helped her into the car and his gentlemanly ways made her wish she could ignore this yearning that Vincenzo had created. She wouldn't give Jesse hope when she knew that all it took from Vincenzo was one look and she was all his. That wasn't right to anyone.

Chapter Eleven

Vincenzo waited inside Arika's apartment, sitting where he had the last time he was there. Seeing her at the restaurant with another guy, he'd wanted to commit fucking murder in front of a room full of witnesses. He was certainly not on a date himself, but gathering information for Galiza, and still he'd not been able to focus on that woman. He didn't date, nor did he take his time like that with a woman. When Galiza asked him to do a job, no matter how much he hated it, he did it. He'd rather kill people than date, but he couldn't pick what to do. After fucking Arika in the bathroom, he'd gone back to the table and finished his meal. When the woman had given him the information he needed, and then asked if he wanted to go back to her place for dessert, he'd told her no.

He'd dropped her off and come straight here.

If she didn't arrive soon, he wasn't going to be held responsible for putting that fucker in the ground. Arika belonged to him, no one else.

At the sound of her keys turning in the door, he waited. She entered seconds later, and he found he was able to relax. Not a hair was out of place and she didn't look like she'd been ravished either.

"You really need to stop breaking into my apartment," she said.

"It's not breaking in if I have a spare key."

She slammed her door closed, and he raised a brow as she locked each bolt until she was secure in her apartment. It was ridiculous to think of the number of bolts on the door keeping her safe. All he needed to do to get inside was throw his weight against the door and he'd be in.

He didn't tell her that because he had an idea that

she already knew it.

"You've got to stop doing this," she said, turning back to face him.

"Doing what?"

"This. It's not fair. You told me it was too dangerous to be part of your life and yet here you are, watching me. Waiting for me. We had sex in a restaurant bathroom, Vincenzo. Doesn't that clue you in to the fact that we need to be careful? That we have to stop doing this?" She pressed her fingers to her head, looking so confused. "I don't even know what you want from me anymore."

He saw the sadness in her eyes as he watched her. She put her bag to one side, and he thought she'd come and sit with him. She went straight for the kitchen. Getting to his feet, he walked the few steps that would take him to her kitchen. Her apartment was so small.

"You need to make a decision," she said, filling a kettle with water.

"This life is not easy."

She put the kettle on the stove. "I get that it's not easy, but you're bringing me into it each time you come to visit and I can't deny you."

"Why not?"

"Don't do that, Vincenzo. You know why."

"Maybe I'd like to hear it."

"You want to hear it, fine? Because I happen to like you. That regardless of how we met, when you touch me, I can't think straight. I don't *want* to think straight. All I want is to be with you. I've never been the kind of woman that would go on a date while screwing another guy on that date. I don't want to be that person. But I can't seem to help myself with you."

"Then what do you want, Arika?"

"I want you to make a decision. To either be part

of my life and accept that you can't seem to stay away from me too, or leave." Her chest was heaving with every single indrawn breath.

She looked positively stunning.

"I don't know what to do anymore," she said. "I … I want you. I'm not going to turn you down. I enjoy what you do to me, and I also like spending time with you. When you were taking care of me, those few weeks were amazing. This isn't because of who you are either. I'm not asking for a lifetime."

"And what if I was?"

"What do you mean?"

"In the mafia, there is no escaping or getting out of it clause. If you're in then you're in for life. That's what I can offer you."

"I just want you, Vincenzo. Not your title or anything else. I just want you. I don't care about what you do. I like you. I know I shouldn't because you're a bad guy, but you're a bad guy to them, not to me. You've never hurt me, and I know you never will."

He rounded the counter and stood right in front of her. Tucking some hair behind her ear, he tilted her head back and stared into her eyes.

"I've never cared about anyone or anything. I bring death to everything I touch, but with you, that didn't happen. I didn't kill you. I protected you. I helped you. I don't want to kill you or to stop seeing you. I've tried that. I've tried to stay away, and I can't. I know to be the better man that I should walk away. Never see you again, but I can't do that. I want you more than anything else in the world, Arika, and for that reason, I'm going to do the selfish thing, and keep you."

With that, he slammed his lips down on hers.

She gasped, moaning as she wrapped her arms around his neck. Reaching past her, he turned the stove off, and then lifted her up in his arms, carrying her to her bedroom. The small apartment space only required a few steps to get to every single location.

Dropping her to the bed, he removed his jacket, stripping down naked before tackling her clothes. She ran her hands up his chest as he got her naked before he shoved her back down to the bed.

Taking hold of her hands, he pressed them above her head, smiling down at her.

"I just want to make one thing clear."

"What?"

"When we're together and you're underneath me, then I'm the one that is in charge. I'm going to be the one to take care of you."

"Okay."

"I want you to quit your job."

She shook her head. "No, that's not going to happen."

"Arika."

"No. You're this big mafia dude and fine, whatever. If something happens to you and I'm left alone, I've got no way to protect myself. I know my apartment's small and that my furniture is on the worn side, but I can afford this. I'm not going to stop working because you want me to."

"Even if I offer to send you to college full-time?"

He saw the temptation there, and she surprised him when she shook her head.

"You don't want that?"

"I'd love that, but I'm not changing my plan. I'm sorry, Vincenzo, but that's the way it has to be. I don't want to quit work. I'm not with you to take care of me. I'm with you because I like you, a lot."

He reached between them, grabbing his dick and sliding it between her wet slit. Bumping her clit, he moved down, finding her entrance and then filling her in one hard thrust, making them both cry out. "It's like you were made for me, baby. All me and no one else."

"Please," she said.

"I'll let you keep your job, but you will live somewhere else." He pulled out of her and slammed in deep again.

"This is my place."

"I will protect you how I see fit. Keep your job, but you will let me protect you. Those locks are not enough."

"Please, Vincenzo, I don't need your protection."

"To be mine, you will do this. I'll let you keep your job, but not this. A compromise."

He saw her grit her teeth.

"My job or my apartment?"

"Yes. I think I'm being rather considerate, don't you?"

"No."

"Well, it's one or the other. Pick." He fucked her hard, watching her struggle to form the words. She was stunning to watch. She belonged all to him. He'd never had a woman that was his before, and he liked it.

"I'll keep my job," she said.

"Good. We'll start hunting for a new place for you tomorrow. For now, I want you to come." He reached between her thighs and started to stroke her, feeling her pussy tighten around him. Her tits shook as he pushed her toward orgasm, and seeing her come apart, that was a sight to behold.

He would do everything in his power to protect her, to keep his world from ever touching her. Nothing could happen to her. When he was with her, she kept his own demons at bay, and that thrilled him more than anything. He'd tried to keep his distance, to not see her.

It hadn't happened. He couldn't stay away.

So now he'd find a way to make a life with her while keeping her safe.

What could possibly go wrong?

****

Arika looked at the third apartment that Vincenzo had dragged her to. Waking up that morning with him still in her bed had been a little surreal. He'd not slept in the same bed as she had when they were together, so she wasn't entirely sure what to make of it.

The real estate agent was yammering away, flirting with him to no end. When they first met up over two hours ago, she'd called her the sister. When Vincenzo had taken her hand, pressed a kiss to her knuckles and said she wasn't his sister but his woman, her stomach had done little flutters. Of course, the woman had looked shocked. Why wouldn't she be?

Arika was the plain woman who'd snagged herself a handsome man.

Keeping her distance, she looked at the large space. There was no furniture in sight. Moving toward the window, she saw the pool at the back where several men, women, and children were already enjoying the weather.

"How much is this place to rent?" she asked, interrupting whatever they'd been taking about.

The agent looked at Vincenzo with a smile. "This is not a rental property."

"I'm not looking to rent something," Vincenzo said, moving toward her, wrapping his arms around her.

"I can only afford rentals. I thought we were clear on that." She had tried this morning to compromise and negotiate what he was spending on her.

She didn't want him to throw away good money if he became bored for whatever reason.

"Arika, I listened, but I didn't pay attention. I want you to have the best. You like the pool?" he asked, looking over her shoulder.

"How much is this to buy?"

The agent gave her an amount that made her jerk back. Vincenzo didn't let her go.

"You can't pay for this. It's ridiculous."

"This is one of the safest areas within the city. The building offers not only security but there's a pool, a game room, and also a small grocery store on the ground floor for your convenience. The cost is all included in the purchase price. There's also a gym."

She thought about Vincenzo working out at his home and the women here drooling all over him. "I won't need a gym."

"Arika, this is the home I want you to have."

"It's too expensive."

"I won't spare any expense when it comes to your safety. Do you like this place?"

She gritted her teeth and turned back to look out of the window.

"Leave us, please. I want to talk with her in private."

"I'll be outside. Take all the time you need."

She heard the woman's heels clicking on the wood floor. The door opened, closed, and then they were alone.

Vincenzo pulled her against him, his arms banding around her waist as his lips nuzzled her neck. "Tell me what the problem is, Arika."

"This is too much. It's too expensive."

"I think it's rather cheap."

"Really? This is ... I know I said you could buy or rent me an apartment, but this goes beyond that. I can't do this on my own if you decide to leave me."

His hold on her tightened. "You really think there's a chance of me wanting to leave you?"

"I don't know. I really don't, but I'm me and you're you. You've probably been with thousands of women. You can have anyone you want."

He sighed. "And yet here I am, willing to spend the rest of my life with you."

This shocked her.

She spun in his arms, staring into his eyes. "A life?"

"You don't think this was only going to be a few passing months, did you?"

"I didn't know what to think. A lifetime is a long time."

"Yes, it is, and I want to spend it with you. Not arguing about where you are. This is a cheap place, but it's in a good area. Low to zero crime rate. You can also walk to the diner. I want to get you a car."

"I can't drive."

"Then I'll pay for lessons. You'll drive to the diner and home. I won't have it any other way. We will also be training you to shoot."

"Wait, what?"

"You'll have your own gun, just in case."

"Vincenzo, this is too much."

"This is what I require. I want this, Arika. I want to be with you. My place, it's not as safe. A lot of shit has gone down there, and I want us to have *our* place, something to call our own. I know you're not after me for my money or shit like that. I get it, Arika. You're not like other women I'm used to. I am who I am so I need to know at all times that you're protected. The only way to do that is to make sure you can take care of yourself."

She glanced over his shoulder. "By learning to shoot a gun?"

"Yes. Don't worry. That's all you'll be taught. I don't need you to get all happy about this. Now, are we going to argue about this, or are you going to listen to me?"

"This is too much."

"Then we'll find another apartment for you. One I will be buying and you'll love. This one could go while you're being a pain in the ass. I've got no problem you being here. It's safe, and I've looked into the security of every single apartment we're looking at today."

She turned back to look down at the pool. The families there looked so happy.

Vincenzo moved past her, opening the door that led out onto the balcony. "Come and look."

He held his hand out, and she gripped it, stepping up beside him, looking down. The pool looked really inviting on this hot day. She was tired of apartment hunting. The place she'd been living in had taken her three months to find. It was perfect for her. This was sheer luxury as far as she was concerned.

"They all look happy."

"You can be happy here too, Arika. I want you to have everything your heart desires."

"I'm not with you for what you can give me."

"I know that, believe me. You not wanting me for my money or my position only makes me want to spoil you even more. You're a gem, and I will take care of you however I can."

She took a deep breath. "Then I do like it here. I prefer it here."

"You're not just saying that?"

"No."

"Good. Stay here while I'll handle the rest."

She watched him leave before leaning on the balcony, staring down below. There were several families running around, squealing and jumping in the pool. All of them were laughing, and she found herself chuckling along with their antics. It did look like a lot of fun.

When one kid threw several girls into the pool, she smiled and stood up.

Stepping back into the apartment, she took a deep breath. This was her home.

Running her fingers against the wall, she stepped into the corridor that led to two bedrooms. Opening one, she went straight to the window, seeing the view overlooking the city.

This space was amazing.

She was walking into the kitchen when Vincenzo came back into the room.

"Where's the woman gone?"

"Signed and sealed. This place is now yours."

"Right now?"

"Yep. We need to go and pack up your apartment."

"We're going to need a big truck to bring my furniture."

"I've already called a place I know. They're going to deliver your furniture here."

"You've given someone else keys to my apartment?" she asked.

He chuckled. "No. You're having new."

"Vincenzo?"

"Nope. I'm not going to hear it. This apartment is a lot bigger than yours. You can be pissed at me, but I promised to take care of you. This is me doing my job the best way I know how." He gripped her hips, pulling her close.

"It's a job?"

"No. Taking care of you is not a job. Not even

close. It's a pleasure." He pressed a kiss to her lips. "This was a new first for me today."

"It was? How?"

"I've never been shopping for an apartment for my woman before."

"You've never been in a relationship?"

"Not once. You're a first."

"That woman at the restaurant?"

"You don't even need to worry about her. She doesn't matter."

"What about other women? I mean, is this going to be exclusive?" She should have probably asked all of this before agreeing to move into an apartment for him to pay for. Arika hadn't wanted to change her apartment, but Vincenzo had convinced her that it would be safer for her protection and if he was worried about her, he wouldn't be able to focus on his job. She didn't want to think of him getting hurt because of her, and she'd realized how unreasonable she'd been with him over sharing an apartment or at least living together. It didn't make this any easier for her though. He didn't want her at his apartment because it wasn't as safe as he wanted it. She didn't want to move in with him yet because of what it made her feel like with him helping her financially. She didn't think she brought much to their relationship as it was. She was so torn over this. She bit her lip, waiting for an answer.

"There's not going to be anyone else but you." He stroked her cheek. "How can you even for a second think that there's someone else in this world that I'd want more than you?"

With that, he dropped his lips against hers and her troubles melted away as if they were nothing.

She could do this.

Have her life and be part of his.

She couldn't give him up. That wasn't an option.

Chapter Twelve

"This is a gun range?" Arika asked.

"Yes. This is where I used to come to practice." Vincenzo climbed out of his car and rounded the vehicle to help her. Heading toward the trunk, he grabbed his case of weapons and locked up his car.

"Do you think it's a good idea for me to be here?"

"Yes. Plenty of women learn to shoot. I won't put you in danger." He took her hand as they made their way inside.

"I wasn't really worrying about that."

"You're just trying to find an excuse to not do this."

"I don't like the thought of handling a gun. They're dangerous, you know. Deadly."

"I know. That's the point. You can still shoot to disarm, not to kill."

"I'd rather not shoot at all." She wrinkled her nose, and he found her utterly charming. Pinching her nose, he pressed a kiss to her lips, playing with her.

"You're cute."

He did the necessary checks before heading toward the back of the shooting range. This place had several different ways of being able to shoot. Rather than take her outside to shoot long range, he'd brought her inside where she could stand in a lane, and he'd be able to show her.

The next best place would be to shoot beer cans in the woods, but he didn't think she'd go for that.

He put the case on the counter, opening it up and taking out a pistol.

"This seems like a waste of bullets."

"Come on, Arika. I need to know you can do this."

Grabbing some ear protection, he placed them on her head and smiled at her. "See, all ready."

She rolled her eyes.

Stepping behind her, he placed her hand on the gun, covering hers with his. There was already a target pinned up waiting.

"Now, I want you to aim for his chest."

"Can't I aim for a shoulder?"

"If something was to ever happen you're going to need to cause maximum damage to give you a chance to get away. A shoulder bullet will hurt, but if the man or men who are coming at you are used to being hit, they could get angry and hurt you even more."

"How about I take the gun and put it against my temple? Me dead stops all that."

He tensed up and placed his lips against her ear. "Do not ever threaten that again, Arika. I mean it. Your death is not something I take very fucking lightly."

"You're angry."

"You just threatened to kill yourself. Of course I'm angry."

"It was just a joke."

"A real fucking lame one. Now, make it up to me and shoot something."

She took a deep breath, aimed, and fired. He held her hands, but she did all the work.

"Good." He pressed the button, and the target came up to them.

She'd hit the space around the target. "Well, I can piss off air."

He removed the target and replaced it with another. "I had my hands on you so it may have affected your targeting." Once everything was back in place, he put his hands on her waist, staying close to her. "Aim for the chest."

She took a deep breath and shot twice.

"Again."

She shot again.

He pressed a button, and the target came into focus. "Were you thinking about me?"

Four bullets were inside the head of the target.

"I was aiming for his stomach."

"Then let's aim for his head this time and see what happens."

For the next hour he kept making her shoot, practice after practice. She'd get some targets that she aimed for, and others just didn't hit the right mark.

He wouldn't let her stop though. This was important.

After five hours of practice, he knew it was time to call it quits. Packing away her targets into the box with his guns, which he'd unloaded, they left the range.

He helped her into the car, and they drove away.

"I didn't like that place. As a date, it sucked big time."

"I had no intention of calling it a date. Are you hungry?" To answer his question, her stomach growled. "I'll take that as a yes."

They passed a drive-thru for burgers and he pulled in, ordering them both some food.

Their order had to wait, and he parked up in one of the available spots. The scent was making his mouth water. He didn't like junk food like this, but for now it would do.

The position they were in, they saw inside the fast food joint. A family sat near a window. A girl no older than three was playing with a pony. A boy with a car and their parents were there too.

It looked like a good family outing, and he glanced over at Arika. For the first time, he saw a little hint of envy in her eyes. "Did you ever want to be adopted?"

"When I was a lot younger and I hadn't been passed over so many times. Whenever new parents would come there was always that nervous excitement within the home, you know. They all wanted the chance at a different life. You never know what could have happened. I think most of the time we all just wanted to be loved."

"Was your foster home not a loving one?"

"It was a good one. I mean, it helped us through a lot of tough times in our life, but it wasn't exactly a place designed to be loving. They were there to do their job. I think it's where I realized that we were work, you know. They were taking care of us, and some of them had homes to go back to. Families. I remember one Christmas when I believed in miracles and Santa and all that stuff. I asked for a family for Christmas. I know, rather lame, but I did. A family that loved me and would take care of me. Anyway, that never happened, and one of the new women that had been working at the home came back in the New Year. I was passing their office, and I happened to hear them talking. She talked about how amazing her Christmas was and what her kids had got and what her husband had got her. She was so happy. Showing pictures and then I heard her say she wished she didn't have to come back to work at times. Then I knew that like a teacher or a receptionist or a secretary or a fireman, she was doing her job. Being paid to take care of us. I think I grew up that year. You?"

"I freaked the fuck out of the system to be honest. I hurt things. Whenever they were around me, they always looked terrified. They even blamed the cat's death on me."

"You killed a cat?"

"No. I didn't kill a cat or a dog or a bunny. I liked to watch insects and occasionally see how they handled having their wings or legs pulled. I also liked playing with knives, and I'd sneak into the kitchen. They found me a few times carving up meat that was to be cooked. I was a freaky fucking kid."

"They're places that are necessary."

"Yes. They are. There were always kids that were full of themselves. How they'd get picked over you. Driving it to you that you were fucking weird and people only wanted perfection. It pissed me off. It's how the Galiza family became alerted to me."

"What do you mean?"

"One of the kids. He liked to tell me how much of a freak I was. One day as he was yelling it at me, I decided to get my own revenge, so I punched his face and started to cut him using my knife. If it makes you feel any better, he was the one responsible for killing the cat. He'd fed it anti-freeze, sick fuck. I tried to stop him, but he'd already done it so I was going to hurt him. That cat was the only thing that came near me that wasn't afraid of me. I loved it when he purred."

"Have you ever thought about getting a cat?" she asked.

"No."

"One day I'd like to have a cat and a puppy, and maybe a bunny as well."

"We'll have to pick them out."

She looked back at the diner. "Do you want a family one day?"

"I don't know, Arika. I really don't know."

He left it at that as their food arrived.

****

"You know you've been in a really good mood lately," Rachel said, making Arika pause.

"I have? I thought I was always in a chipper mood."

"Nah, this is something else. You know. You're a lot happier. You normally looked miserable, or at least bored with life. You're smiling a lot more now than ever before. It's good. It's a good look on you." Rachel winked at her.

She couldn't say anything else as they had a full diner tonight. The food was flowing, and there was laughter everywhere. It was a good night, a fun one. After collecting food, she walked between the tables, filling up their drinks, taking plates away, cleaning up tables so new families could come and eat.

At around eight in the evening the entire diner went silent, and she turned toward the door seeing three men she didn't recognize entering the diner.

"That's the Vitale family."

"I thought they were all dead."

"The Galizas wiped them out."

"A war. A bloodbath."

At the mention of Galiza, she felt nervous.

They, of course, sat in her section, which was just great. Putting the coffeepot back in place, she glanced over her shoulder. They were looking at the menu.

"This is fucking scary," Rachel said.

"What is?"

"The Vitales being here."

"Who are they?"

"They're part of the mafia."

"How is it you guys know all about this?"

"When you live on the streets you learn who to steer clear of. Believe me, they're one of them. People talk, Arika. If you went out more, you'd hear and know more. Them being here is really bad. Those two guys a few months ago, they're part of another family. This is bad, real bad."

Instead of letting nerves get the better of her, Arika grabbed her order pad and approached them.

She hadn't been worried or scared to serve Vincenzo and his friend. It didn't matter that she didn't know who they were at the time and it was only during the night that she heard the whispers and rumors. Of course, she had a nice scar in her abdomen from Daniel's handiwork.

"Hi, I'm Arika. I'll be your waitress this evening. What can I get you?" she asked, pen poised ready to write.

They ignored her and kept looking at the menu.

"What is good here, Arika?"

"Tonight's specials are the fish soup, the house burgers, and the meat pies. Also, the strawberry cream pie for dessert."

They sighed, and she waited.

She hoped Vincenzo didn't choose this night to show up. He didn't visit her at her place of work, but, seeing as she was struggling to learn to drive, he sometimes picked her up, or at least sent a cab her way.

After taking their orders, she immediately left and placed them at the kitchen.

"Be careful," Frank, the owner, said.

"I will."

"No, Arika. I've not said anything about that man who came to see me about you, but I know he and the Vitales are not a good mix," Frank said.

"What do you want me to do?" she whispered to her boss.

"You need to tell him in some way that they're here. I don't like it."

She glanced around the diner and saw several families had already gotten up to leave. The mere presence of the Vitales had sent people scurrying. She didn't like this. "I'll call him."

Leaving the kitchen, she made her way to the staffroom, being careful to not look in their direction. She didn't want to alert them to what she'd been asked to do. She didn't even want to think about why her boss was asking her to do this.

She went to her bag, grabbed her cell phone, and started to dial Vincenzo's number. Her hands were shaking.

He'd given her all the numbers she could contact him on along with the best ways of getting a hold of him. She had Daniel's contact information as well. She didn't want to call Daniel. Since she and Vince had been going together, she'd not seen anything of Daniel. Vincenzo did say he would do everything he could to make sure his life didn't touch her. She gathered that also meant killing people.

"Arika, what's wrong?" Vincenzo asked after a couple of rings.

"My boss asked me to call. Some Vitale men are here. I don't know what any of that means."

"Vitale men?"

"Yes, my boss recognized them, I think. He wants you to come."

She heard him curse over the line.

"Listen to me very carefully, Arika. I want you to grab your bag and leave. Don't make a scene. Just leave and get as far away from there as possible."

"I can't do that. I've got friends here. We've got families here. What does this mean?"

"Damn it! Don't argue with me over this."

"I'm not going to leave Rachel here on her own. No, I won't do that. I'm staying here. I just thought you should know."

"I can't fucking protect you. I'm across town."

"Then let's hope they're only here to eat." With that, she hung up and left the staffroom, going back into the kitchen where her boss was waiting. "I called him."

"And?"

"We wait." She wasn't going to tell him that Vincenzo couldn't be there. "We're just going to have to serve them and live with it."

"They're driving my customers away."

"Then serve them pronto so we can move them along." She'd never spoken to her boss like that, but right now she wasn't in the mood to be ordered around. She got that Vincenzo wanted to protect her, but she wasn't going to leave her friends or innocent people. Heading back into the main diner, she saw more people had left.

Fortunately, no more mafia men had turned up, and as she grabbed the coffeepot, she began to make the rounds. Putting a smile on her face, she stopped at a couple of tables, asking them how they were enjoying their meal, if they wanted dessert, and just being friendly, trying to put them at ease.

Frank rang up their order, and Rachel was in the furthest corner of the diner.

Grabbing the Vitales' food, Arika kept a smile on her face and served them. "If there's anything else, let me know."

"Actually, we were curious about something."

She stopped, waiting. "What about?"

"We were wondering if a couple of men stopped by here a few weeks ago. Both tall, one of them blond, the other had black hair."

"We get a lot of customers through that door with blond or black hair." Daniel had blond hair. Vincenzo had black. "I'm sorry. Are you missing them or something?"

"They would have been wearing expensive, Italian-made suits."

"Again, you're asking the wrong girl."

"What about the other one working tonight?"

"I don't know. You'd have to ask her. This is my section though. Please enjoy your meal and let me know if you need anything else."

Stepping away, she kept on doing her job, not exactly sure how she could keep her composure. Everything seemed to be crashing down around her. She had noticed the pieces they were carrying.

Why bring a gun to a damn diner?

Time ticked by and people left. The Vitales didn't ask for extra, and after an hour they were finished and packing up. She watched them stand, ready to leave. She breathed out a sigh of relief, and that was quickly gone when the door opened.

Turning to see who it was, she saw Vincenzo, Daniel, and a couple of other men, all of them with deadly expressions on their face.

Before she could say or do anything, she heard the sound of guns being cocked. Looking toward the men, they were already drawn and ready.

Everything happened so fast. Shots rang out, and Vincenzo was on her, shoving her to the ground as glasses smashed around her. "Stay the fuck down."

She nodded and curled in a ball as she heard the screams and shouts.

Rolling over onto her stomach, she shuffled from around the counter where she'd been when all the mess was starting. She saw Rachel on the ground, her body still.

"Rachel!"

Her friend wasn't moving.

Crawling across shattered glass, Arika saw there

was a gunshot near Rachel's throat. She was bleeding out.

"No! No! No! Someone, call an ambulance. Come on, Rachel. You're fine. You're fine." She pressed her hand to the spot, but there wasn't even a flinch or a gasp for breath.

Rachel was dead.

Tears sprang to her eyes, and she pressed her face against Rachel's chest, feeling immense pain.

The diner no longer looked like her place of work. It looked like a bloodbath. The few remaining families that had been there were cowering under the tables, and a few bodies were on the floor.

This wasn't supposed to happen.

She shouldn't have called Vincenzo.

"Babe," Vincenzo said. "She's gone. You need to let her go."

"She needs a doctor."

"Arika, she's dead."

"No. Get an ambulance."

"Dude, you're going to have to knock her the fuck out so we can deal with this."

"Shut up, Daniel."

"You know what needs to happen. She's fucking panicking."

"Babe, look at me."

"She needs an ambulance. Get her one."

"I'm so sorry about this."

Suddenly she was grabbed, a hand covering her mouth. She tried to fight it, but everything went dark.

Chapter Thirteen

"You did what you had to do, Vince. Don't look so worried."

Vincenzo ignored Daniel as he stared at the woman in his lap. Arika had been panicking, not thinking about what she was doing. Her friend had died, a gunshot wound to her throat in the crossfire.

Vitale had been on their turf.

Getting the call from Arika, he'd dropped everything he was doing, the meeting he had with Galiza, to come to her aid. Fear for her safety had been his only concern, so much so that he told Galiza he had to go to her. Before he could leave, his boss had asked him what was so important about this woman, and he'd told him straight that he loved her.

There was going to be a conversation between them very soon, but until then, Galiza had said for him to take backup. Vitales had been growing in recent weeks, and it was time they learned their place once again.

"I promised her this life wouldn't touch her."

"Then you shouldn't have made that promise, man. None of us can guarantee shit like that. It's impossible to do. We can only hope that we keep our families safe." Daniel looked at him in the rearview mirror. "Boss knows now. At least you don't have to keep going around sneaking past shit."

"She can't go back to the diner."

"There's not much of a fucking diner left."

"Frank will be compensated. So will Rachel's family," he said.

When he'd seen the guns, he'd acted on instinct, drawing his weapon and firing as he pushed Arika to the ground. He couldn't allow anything to happen to her. She was his entire world.

Daniel pulled up outside of his suburban home. He figured it would be best to bring her to a place that she liked. His home was that place.

"Do you want some help?" Daniel asked.

"No."

Opening the door, he picked her up in his arms, carrying her into his home. Closing the door, he quickly flicked the lock into place and took her upstairs. Resting her on the bed, he saw there was blood on her hands and knees. She'd crawled through broken glass to get to her friend.

She was still out for the count and would be for a while.

Knocking his opponent unconscious in a neck hold had been a skill he practiced as not everyone carried chloroform on their person, and no one knew when they'd need it.

Carrying her through to the bath, he lowered her into the tub. "I never wanted any of this to happen to you, babe." He removed her uniform and was careful as he filled the tub. He grabbed his first aid kit and started to clean out the glass. Some shards were in her knees, and he didn't like that she could be in any kind of pain.

Piece by piece, he cleaned her up, scrubbing off the day until she was as good as new, at least in body.

Lifting her up again, he carried her through to the bedroom. He put one of his shirts on her, to help before putting a few bandages to cover the worst of the cuts.

Once that was done, he put her into bed.

Taking a seat on the chair, he stared over at her.

Never in all of his life had he ever been more terrified than thinking about her alone and vulnerable at the Vitale men's mercy.

He'd been talking with Galiza, making him see sense about who was responsible for the raids, missing shipments, and also the attacks on the clubs.

He understood that his boss didn't want to think that his own son would betray him. Vincenzo wasn't lying though. The pictures didn't lie, and neither had the reporter. He'd been given the information by none other than Galiza's youngest son, Rafe. As far as Vincenzo was concerned, Rafe had always been a loose cannon. He was a spoiled bastard who thought the world owed him everything and that he was the one who should be leading. It just didn't work that way. Being the youngest son, he was at the bottom of the fucking food chain.

His jealousy of his father but also of his older brothers knew no bounds. During Vincenzo's search, he had uncovered Rafe's attempt to kill his oldest brother, Antonio, as well. There had been three attempts on Antonio's life, and he'd even lost his girlfriend in the process as well.

Rubbing at his eyes, Vincenzo felt so fucking tired.

Not only did they have Rafe's betrayal, there was also the alliance he'd started with the Vitales. His meeting with Gabe had been eye-opening.

The Vitale family was divided. Those that followed the father didn't follow the son. According to Gabe, the son, Benjamin Vitale, wanted peace. He wanted an alliance with Galiza, to bring their families together and to make them great once again. The father, however, Benjamin Vitale, senior—they liked to keep all the names within the family, which was why Vincenzo struggled to fucking remember them all—wanted war. He wanted to tear down the Galiza family, to become a leader all on his own. To have the streets run red with blood and for the power to be back in his shitty hands.

Vincenzo now had to create a meeting between Galiza and Benjamin Vitale to come to an understanding with regards to Rafe and the senior Benjamin.

To add all of that pressure, he was also worried about his woman. She had lost her friend tonight, and there was no way in hell that wasn't going to bite him in the ass. He didn't want this for her. Far from it.

Getting to his feet, he brushed a curl behind her ear.

"You will never know how sorry I am that I failed you tonight."

He left the room, needing a stiff drink.

Grabbing his whiskey, he poured himself a glass just as there was a knock on his door. Instantly, he had his gun by his side, ready.

No one came to his suburban house.

No one fucking knew him.

He moved slowly toward the door, being careful not to make a sound. Checking through the peephole, he saw it was Antonio Galiza, the oldest son.

He opened the door and glared at the man. "What the fuck are you doing here?"

"I came to see you, obviously."

"How did you know where I lived?"

"It's not that hard to know what you do and who you do, Barbato. We may not be close, but I think it's important to know where all my father's minions live and breathe. May I come in, or would you like to do this on your doorstep when anyone could be watching?"

Seeing no other choice, Vincenzo pulled back the door to let him in. The moment he closed the door, he pressed the barrel of the gun against the man's temple. "If you try anything, I will fucking end you." "You kill me and my dad will hunt you down like a dirty fucking dog. I'm not here to hurt you, Vincenzo. Not even close. You can put the gun away."

"Then why are you here? This is my home."

"I know. It's rather … homey."

"Why don't you tell me what you want?"

"My father told me what happened with Rafe. The accusations and also the evidence you have on him. He's the one that made us aware of the reporter."

"Your father doesn't like the truth."

"My father doesn't like to know that he raised a weak son, and in Rafe that is what has happened. He was a premature baby, so my mother babied him for a long time. He would scream the fucking house down even as a child. A pain in the ass. I wanted to smother him when he was sleeping. A couple of times I even held the pillow in my hand, prepared to deal with him. I should have done it."

"You didn't."

"I believe you, and I know that Rafe is not going to let this go. Even if Father punishes him."

"What do you want me to do?" Vincenzo asked.

"When the time comes, I'm going to need you to pull the trigger."

"This is not going to be handled the Galiza way?"

"He's Mom's favorite, and Dad made a promise that he would do everything to keep her sons safe. Not that she has much of a choice in these matters."

"I don't work for you, Antonio. I may have stopped the attempts to kill you, but that doesn't make us friends."

"I never expected us to be friends. Far from it. I wanted you to know I'm on your side."

"Is that all?"

"Yes." Antonio held his hand out. "Thank you. I happen to like living and breathing."

Vincenzo wanted to ignore that hand. He and Antonio had never seen eye to eye on a lot of things. When he'd been taken in by Galiza, Antonio had hated him.

Still, the past was in the past.

Shaking Antonio's hand, he nodded at him. He would protect Galiza no matter what, even if he didn't like the ugly old bastard.

****

Arika woke to the scent of bacon frying and the memory of Rachel dead.

Staring down at her body, in one of Vincenzo's shirts, she knew he'd taken care of her uniform. He'd probably even burned it.

Pushing her hand through her hair, she climbed out of bed and went to his bathroom. He'd brought her to his suburban home, the place he came when he was taking care of her last time.

She finished on the toilet, washed her hands, brushed her teeth, and stared at her reflection. She looked defeated.

Lifting up the shirt, she stared at her reflection, at the gunshot wound from months ago.

Thinking about the sounds of bullets, she closed her eyes, flinching as she saw Rachel's dead body. A hole in the side of her neck where her throat should have been.

Dropping her shirt, she stepped back from the mirror and went in search of Vincenzo.

He was standing in the kitchen, frying bacon.

"I heard you get up," he said. "Did you sleep well?"

"You knocked me out."

"I didn't hit you."

"How did you do it then?"

"I cut off your air supply enough for you to lose consciousness. Then I guess you fell asleep."

"She's dead."

"Yes."

"Why did they start shooting?" she asked. "I don't understand why they did that. Everything was fine. They were going to leave."

"They wanted to start a war. It's what they do. Rachel got caught in the crossfire."

"I should have made her leave with me. I should have left and made her leave and the people and I should have done something."

"It wouldn't have mattered what you did, Arika. They were going to cause trouble there. It's why they went fully loaded. They were going to shoot up the place."

"Why?"

"Because they could. Because that's what the Vitales do."

"They were asking about you," she said.

"What?"

"They asked if a blond-haired man and black-haired man had been there. Described your suits."

"They were looking to leave their mark."

She wrapped her arms around herself.

He stepped closer, coming toward her. She didn't pull away as he wrapped his arms around her, holding her close. "I didn't want this to happen to you. I know you're angry and upset, and I'm so sorry you had to see that last night."

She couldn't hold back. Hugging him close, she held onto him, not wanting to let him go. "I was so afraid."

"I know."

"Are you angry with me?"

"No. I'm not angry with you. I failed you last night. I should have been there, and I wasn't."

"It's not your fault. What's going to happen now?

The diner, the people, what?"

"Galiza has people within the police force. They're going to take care of it. The people that were hurt will get compensated, but it will be known as another gang war gone wrong."

"It's crazy to think what's going on." She pulled away, gripping his shirt.

"You won't be going back to the diner."

She tilted her head back, looking at him. "Last I saw there wasn't much of a diner." She bit her lip. "I can't stop seeing her."

"It'll get easier." He ran his hands up and down her arms.

"What happens now?"

"Well, this isn't over."

"What do you mean?"

"You called when I was dealing with business. Last night I told my boss that I was seeing you. He wants to meet you."

"He does?"

"Yes."

"Does that have to happen?"

"It really does," he said.

She closed her eyes and took another deep breath. "You don't do things by halves, do you?"

He took hold of her hands, clasping them together. "I realized something last night. I had a feeling that it was that way, but I didn't know for certain until there was a risk that you could die last night."

"This is really not romantic."

"I realized that I love you, Arika."

As far as revelations go, this one was right up there. She was shocked.

"You love me?"

"Yes. I love you, and I know that if anything was

to happen to you, the street wouldn't be able to handle the kind of war I would create to seek justice for your death."

"I'm not dead." She was still reeling from the fact he loved her. "I ... you love me?"

"Yes. More than anything else in the world. When all of this is over, I'm going to marry you. A good man would walk away. He'd let you have a life that you deserve. I'm not a good man. I can't walk away. I want you to myself, and I don't want to share you with anyone."

"Shouldn't you get down on one knee? Propose properly?"

"Soon. I will soon." He kissed her cheek. "You need to eat something."

He pulled out a chair, patting the seat. She sat down as he went to serve their food.

"What did you mean when you said about this all being over? It's not over?"

"No. I've got to deal with some business first. After we've eaten breakfast I'm taking you to Galiza's home. There you will be safe while I deal with some of the work I need to do."

She didn't like the sound of that.

Staring down at the plate of food, heavy with bacon and eggs, the thought of eating made her feel sick.

"You've got to eat something, babe. I need you to be strong for me right now." He took hold of her hand, and she stared at his.

She couldn't stop seeing Rachel's face.

Looking at Vincenzo, she saw the love he had for her shining in his eyes. He'd never shown her that before. He'd always been guarded when he looked at her, but now, he was wide open and she saw everything he hid from her.

"I love you, babe. I wish I could take away what happened last night, but I can't. I need to be able to make this right. Tell me what to do."

"There's nothing you can do. This wasn't your fault." As much as she wanted to blame him, she knew without a doubt that the Vitales had hit first. They'd caused last night's destruction, and in doing so it woke her up.

The mafia had a place in the world and they were horrible, but there were families that tried to keep the streets clean. When Vincenzo and Daniel entered the diner that first night, there had been whispers but nothing to the extent there were about the Vitale men. Her boss had been scared. She'd seen the fear in his eyes, and Rachel had kept her distance from them. Everyone but herself had been afraid.

The Vitale men were the worse of two evils.

Picking up her fork, she forced herself to eat something. She couldn't starve herself. The first bite wasn't so bad, and she finished the entire breakfast.

Vincenzo had also made her a cup of coffee, which she sipped through.

His cell phone started to ring, and she watched him answer. Excusing herself, she walked back upstairs to his room.

She'd not been back here in a long time. Everything was the same as when she left, not a thing out of place.

Going to his drawers, she opened one and found his boxer briefs. When she'd been there before, she hadn't even given a thought to sneaking through his things to see what he had.

So, one by one she opened up his drawers, seeing his ordered boxer briefs and socks. Several drawers were empty, nothing inside them.

"Did you find what you were looking for?"

"You've got drawers empty. Why?"

"I don't need to fill them. I have enough of everything that I need."

Stepping away from his drawers, she stood in his closet. Again, order; suits lined up, everything neat and in place. Nothing out of the ordinary.

"You're a neat freak."

"I like to be able to find everything." He wrapped his arms around her, pulling her against him.

He surrounded her, and she loved his hands on her. The way he comforted her. He worked for monsters and was one himself, and yet she wasn't terrified of him.

His lips brushed against her neck. "Tell me what you're thinking?"

"That there's nowhere else I'd like to be than right here with you. I know that you'll protect me. Keep me safe."

"I'll protect you with my very life."

One of his hands moved to her hips. Her body heated at his touch, feeling the hard length of his cock press against her ass. Even after everything that happened last night, she wanted him.

Reaching behind her, she cupped his dick, and smiled as he hissed. "You're playing with fire there."

"You're turned on. You're hard right now."

"I can't help it. Seeing you in my clothes, having you in my life, being around you, Arika, it weakens me because right now, all I can see is you."

She covered his hand with her own and then pushed his hands between her thighs, closing her eyes as pleasure struck her. She wanted him. "Then take me, Vincenzo. I'm yours to be taken."

Chapter Fourteen

Vincenzo held Arika's hand as he drove onto Galiza's estate. All morning he'd made her come a total of five times as he drove his cock in deep. He'd needed to hear her scream and beg for him not to stop. The last thing he ever wanted to do was to hurt her, and seeing her breaking apart, shattering at his feet with Rachel's body, had cut him deep.

She squeezed his hand, and he caught sight of Daniel waiting.

Arika didn't tense up this time.

He parked the car, climbed out, and Arika waited for him to open the door. He knew it would be a struggle for her to walk as he hadn't gone easy on her. He'd wanted her to remember him, to feel every single inch of his cock as he drove inside her, taking her pussy, claiming her once again as his own.

"You're late."

"I had business to attend to."

"Galiza's waiting inside. I see you didn't keep her a secret for long."

"I didn't want to," he said. She wasn't a secret he was ashamed of. He'd only wanted to keep everything quiet to give her a chance at a normal life. Of course, the moment he decided to be a selfish bastard, he should have told Galiza then.

As he took hold of Arika's hand, they made their way up the stairs into his boss's house.

"Don't be nervous. You're safe here."

"It's fine. I'm fine. Of course I'm fine."

He kissed her cheek.

Antonio was the first person he saw. "Dad's in his office. He's expecting you."

"Arika, I'd like you to meet Antonio. Antonio,

this is my fiancée, Arika."

"Nice to meet you, Arika," Antonio said.

"We're not officially engaged," she said, lifting her head and smiling. "You've not properly asked me."

"You know, I like this one already. You give him hell, Arika. He needs it."

She held his hand a little tighter.

"Daniel, you don't need to go in there. It's just Dad and Vincenzo with his woman."

Walking down the long corridor, he wrapped his arm around Arika.

"Is that bad that we're going in there alone?"

"It's not bad. Believe me. This is private, and I knew you wouldn't want a big family introduction."

"I could just go home, you know. Not worry."

"Once everything is done, we'll go home."

Knocking on the door, he called out his name.

"Come in," Galiza said.

He went in first and then allowed Arika to enter.

"Ah, Vincenzo is here at last. I was beginning to think you were ditching me."

"Something came up this morning."

"I'm aware of what happened at the diner last night. My apologies on your friend's death," Galiza said.

She nodded. "Thank you."

"So, you're the woman that has stolen Vincenzo's heart. A lot of women will be upset about that."

"I'm sorry," she said.

Galiza chuckled. "I have no problem with that. Will you look at me, Arika?"

She lifted her head.

"You're nervous."

"Yes."

"Afraid I'll kill you?"

Vincenzo didn't like this one bit.

"Yes."

"I won't kill you. That is not my way, unless of course you betray me. Has Vincenzo made you aware of the consequences of you talking or betraying us?"

"Yes, he warned me some time ago."

"And yet you're still with him?"

She looked at him this time. "I guess some things can't be denied."

"You love him?" Galiza asked.

She didn't look away and nodded her head. "Yes. I tried not to. I tried to hate him, but it just wasn't working. He's rather hard to hate."

Vincenzo cupped her cheek. "I love you too."

She pressed her face against his open palm.

"I do find this rather a treat, it has to be said," Galiza said. "Vincenzo is like a son to me, and as I look at him now, I've never seen him be so smitten with a woman. For that reason alone, I want this wedding to go ahead. You will be Vincenzo's bride, Arika."

"I don't get a say in this?" she asked.

"Are you saying you don't wish to be married to him?"

"It's not that."

"Then what is it?" Galiza asked.

"I … erm … I'd like him to ask me. To get down on one knee and ask."

Galiza burst out laughing. "They always want to get us by the balls. Well, in that case, Vincenzo, I will leave that to you, but we have business to attend, so hurry up."

His boss left the office.

He was alone with Arika.

"He's terrifying."

"I thought he was one of the coolest men I knew growing up."

"Now?"

"Now, he's just my boss."

"You don't care for him?"

"I care, but I know my place in this world. He says I'm like a son to him, but if given the choice, he'd kill me to keep Antonio alive."

She gripped his hand even tighter. "I don't want you to die, Vincenzo. I can't … no, I don't want that."

"I'm damn good at what I do, and I keep Antonio alive even when I don't want to." He dropped a kiss to her lips. "I'm so sorry about rushing you on this. I don't want to, I swear, but I've got to go."

"You're going to leave me here?"

"I don't have a choice. I've got a job to do, but the women are here. I'll take you to them now. They're probably in the kitchen waiting to meet you."

"Do these women like you?"

"I've been around them a lot. They know how this world works, so they'll let you know what to expect. Don't believe everything you hear."

"Because that's not scary."

"They will take care of you." He stroked her cheek. "I'll be back as soon as I can." He saw how nervous she was and kissed her lips. "Come on. I'll take you to them."

He held her hand and led her through the house to the kitchen where she would see a lot of women talking, cooking, baking. They all looked tense but happy. He was used to them like this. Especially when they were about to go and deal with not only an internal problem but also their enemies. There was a risk that people would die today. He had no intention of dying.

When he cleared his throat, they turned toward him. Galiza's wife didn't even look at him, but she hated this life.

Her sister, the aunt he'd never had, took the lead, smiling and coming toward them.

"This is her?" Aunt Shauna asked.

"Yep. This is Arika, the special woman in my life. Take care of her," he said.

"We will. We're making ciabatta, so she can help."

He took Arika's hands, smiled at her, and handed her over to Aunt Shauna, knowing she'd be safe.

"I'll be back." With that, he turned his back, and started to walk away, heading outside to where Daniel and the rest of the men were waiting for him.

"I can't believe this is going to happen today," Daniel said, climbing behind the wheel.

"It has to happen. You know that. If he doesn't do anything it'll make him look weak, and we can't have him looking weak, not now." Vincenzo glanced back at the house. He was doing the right thing, he knew he was.

****

"You're the first woman Vincenzo has brought around here," Aunt Shauna said.

"I am?"

"Yes. I know that means you're special, and I will keep on hoping for a better life for him rather than the one he's been trained to do."

Arika watched as the woman crossed her chest as if she was praying. "You don't think he's fit for this life?"

"I believe Vincenzo is more than fit for the life of the killer they've made him. I just don't think he had to be that way."

"He told me how Galiza found him. At the foster home."

"That nonsense. Yes, he was a ... strange boy, but there was also a lot of good in him as well. Of course,

Galiza saw the opportunity to create the beast of a man he always wanted, and Vincenzo can do everything so easily."

"Vincenzo is a monster," said a pale woman, who was drinking some dark amber liquid that she guessed was whiskey.

"That's Annette. She's Galiza's wife," Shauna said. "My sister."

"I don't get why you can always keep defending him. He's a monster who'll burn in hell."

"You can stop spilling your vile curses right now, dear sister. We wouldn't all be here if it wasn't for Vincenzo. You should be spitting that nonsense at your son. The one that caused all this mess. You spent way too long babying him to make him believe he was something special, and now we all know what he's capable of. He wanted to kill Antonio, take his place, murder him."

"No, I won't believe it. My Rafe is not capable of such nastiness. He's special. His father spills lies to have me turn against him."

"Forgive my sister, she's a little … different. You're safe here though. Galiza keeps her under control. He has no choice. Before they left, he told us what happened. Until then, it had been a secret. Rafe was never a good boy. Always doing bad things, but she considered him her angel. How wrong she was."

Washing her hands, Arika got introduced to the art of making bread, every now and then seeing Galiza's wife spitting and cursing as she drank the entire bottle of whiskey. After an hour or two, she passed out, and the conversation between the women picked up again, acting as if nothing had happened. This was the life she'd have to get used to.

****

"Well, if it's not dear old Daddy, his fucking

minion, and my brother come to save the day. I see you're still alive," Rafe said.

He was tied to a chair, waiting for what was coming to him.

Vincenzo stayed back as Galiza approached his young son. Antonio's arms were folded as if trying to control himself so he didn't strike back.

"Shut your fucking mouth," Galiza said.

"Oh, Daddy's going all macho, playing the role of who is boss."

"You didn't think you could plot to kill me, take out your brother, bring back the Vitale scum, and get away with it."

"Oh, I planned to bring war back to the streets, to have a little fun before it was over. Tell me, Dad, how are you going to tell Mom about my demise, huh? You're going to let her know how you chained me up like a dog?"

"You're not being chained up like a dog," Vincenzo said. "We let them roam free."

"Ah, the little bitch speaks," Rafe said. "The piece of shit that stopped my evil plan. Tsk, tsk, tsk. I could have turned you into a god."

"No, you couldn't. I don't work for weak men."

Rafe glared at him.

"We want to know everything you've told the Vitale clan."

"I've got nothing to say." He spat at his father, to which Galiza struck out at him.

Rafe burst out laughing.

"Vincenzo, get started," Galiza said, stepping back.

Still, Rafe was laughing.

Daniel brought over his tool kit and placed it near him.

To start, Vincenzo didn't use any tools other than his fists, drawing blood as he wiped the smirk off Rafe's face. The fucker wasn't laughing any longer now.

When the time came for him to start cutting, he made a few slashes against his wrists, watching him bleed a bit before Rafe told them everything they needed to know. That he'd spoken with the father of the Vitale clan, how they intended to rule together, and also the agreements he had in place. Considering the shitstorm he'd created, Rafe hadn't done so much to change their deals, just attempting to divert power to himself when the time was up.

Vincenzo held the gun in his hand, staring at Galiza to give the final order.

"Antonio," Galiza said.

"Yes, sir."

"Deal with this traitor the way we know how."

"What will you tell Mother?" Rafe asked, gasping. The cockiness was gone, the pain clear in his voice.

"I'll tell her that it's not a woman's place to ask questions and to get the fuck on with taking care of the rest of our kids," Galiza said. "You tried to kill your brother, to bring down the Galiza family, to bring more power to our enemies, and the cost of that is death. Antonio, as he attempted to kill you, you may do this."

Vincenzo watched as Antonio raised the gun and shot Rafe in the head three times.

This problem was no more.

Now, to deal with the Vitale problem, and then move on.

****

Later that night, Arika flicked through the pages of the book beside Vincenzo's bed. It was a cookbook and staring at food now made her nervous. She'd enjoyed a large bowl of soup and bread before coming up to get ready for bed. Aunt Shauna was one hell of a strong woman. She'd put her sister to bed and kept all the women in line.

Running fingers through her hair, Arika got up from her bed and moved toward the window. Vincenzo's room looked out over the backyard. She saw several guards walking the grounds.

This life, it seemed so scary and yet full of family. She was in no doubt that it was filled with ugliness, death, and pain. She'd seen a part of that when they took Rachel's life, and of course when she got shot.

She wondered how Vincenzo was. How he was feeling. What he was doing.

Staring across the yard, she tensed as she heard the door open, and there Vincenzo stood, only he wasn't happy.

Arika stayed near the window as he came into the bedroom, shutting the door.

"You're still here," he said.

"Why wouldn't I be?"

"I figured Annette would have pushed you away if given the chance."

"Shauna wouldn't let her." She took a step toward him and saw blood on his shirt and the devastation on his face. "What's going on, Vincenzo?"

"We lost a few men tonight. Daniel was one of them."

"Oh, no," she said, moving up to him.

She threw her arms around him, and he held her tightly. Closing her eyes, she felt his pain and grief, even as he tried to hide it. "I'm so sorry you're going through this."

"I didn't even like him most of the time, but he didn't deserve this. He didn't deserve to die. He was a good man. A shit shot, but a good man."

"What will happen?"

"He didn't have any family. We'll bury him as the soldier he was for his loyalty. He didn't die slowly. It was quick."

"What happened?"

"We went into Vitale land, and as we were negotiating with the son, the father decided to take us out. Rafe had warned him what was going on. We were not prepared. We lost a lot of men tonight. Galiza was shot, but it was a mere flesh wound. It'll be okay."

She cupped his face. "Were you hurt?"

"No."

"Then I'm happy." She pressed a kiss to his lips, but he pulled away. "Vincenzo?"

"I would understand if you wouldn't want any part of this life. If you'd like me to give you a clean break. I can do this. I can make sure no one else will find you. That you can live your life far away from me."

Tears filled her eyes, and she shook her head. "This isn't a proposal."

"No, I'm offering to set you free."

"Then keep it because I don't want any part of it. You can think and be what you like, but it doesn't change the fact that I love you, Vincenzo. I know this life isn't how I imagined. I tried living without you, but I can't. I don't want to. So I'll take the bad with the good. Isn't that all marriages?"

"You want to be with me?"

"Well, you keep telling me that I'm going to marry you, but your proposals need a lot of work."

He cupped her face, slamming his lips down on hers. "I love you, Arika. I love you more than anything else in the world, and I want to spend the rest of my life with you, loving you, taking care of you. Please, marry me."

"Yes. Seeing as you asked so nicely."

She wrapped her arms around his neck, and he picked her up, carrying her through to the shower. She didn't ask any questions, kissing him back with a passion.

There were always sacrifices to be made in this life. He was hers, and she would gladly go to the ends of the earth to be with him, to keep him close, to love him. She pushed his clothes off his body, and as they stepped into the shower, she wrapped her legs around his waist, crying out as he filled her, taking the pleasure he needed from her body.

She moaned with each thrust of his cock, aching for more, wanting him more than anything else.

This wasn't the life she'd imagined, nor was being his wife, but it would be the life she embraced for him. To everyone else, he was a killer, the mafia's personal beast, but to her, he was everything. They saw past each other's flaws, and just saw each other, and for her that was more than enough.

Epilogue

Five years later

Vincenzo looked out into the yard, and his breath was absolutely taken from him. Arika walked across the lawn wearing the white summer dress that so much reminded him of their wedding day. Even though she'd wanted a small wedding, Galiza wouldn't allow that. So they'd had a huge wedding, involving family, friends, and of course the Vitale to show their new alliance to the leader.

The day itself had been a bit of blur, getting to the church and waiting for Arika to arrive. When she spoke, everything was in focus. All he saw was the woman he loved, and the rest of the world fell away. He spoke his vows to her, promising her his life, his everything, and she offered him the same. They'd come together against all odds, and now, five years later, he watched his heavily pregnant wife, walking across their lawn with his son and his daughter.

Daniel and Rachel.

He'd wanted to name his son after the friend he didn't even realize he had.

Sipping his coffee, he left the kitchen, and stood out onto the patio.

"Daddy!" His children's squeals of delight as they charged toward him were worth every single late night with them.

Arika placed a hand on her stomach. "Even this one got a kick out of that."

He held both his kids, and placed a hand to her stomach, touching his baby, feeling her kick.

"She's a little fighter. Just like her mother."

Letting go of her stomach, he cupped her cheek and brought her close. "I love you so damn much," he said, slamming his lips down on hers.

She moaned as their babies groaned and ran off onto the lawn, skipping and dancing as they went.

"You've made me the happiest man alive," he said. "Do you have any regrets?"

"None at all. You?"

"What can I have regret about when you've given me a family, a place in this world, and of course, a reason to keep on fighting?" Not only did they have their family, but Arika had completed her college degree and also ran a foster home for children. Galiza had been more than happy to fund it as he knew it was special to the two of them, and over the years they had showed their loyalty to him.

With his hands on her stomach, Vincenzo kissed her neck, watching their children play. This was what he always wanted. He'd simply had to wait for the right woman, and Arika was that woman. In the person everyone had overlooked, he'd seen his soulmate.

The End

www.samcrescent.com

BESTSELLING BBW ROMANCE
SPICY ROMANCE FOR REAL WOMEN